TOBY TRIED TO EXPLAIN THAT HE HAD ONLY
LEFT THE WAGON TO WASH HIS FACE

TOBY TYLER
OR TEN WEEKS
WITH A CIRCUS
JAMES OTIS

ILLUSTRATED BY
RICHARD H RODGERS

GROSSET & DUNLAP, *Publishers* NEW YORK

By arrangement with Harper & Brothers

CONTENTS

CHAP.   PAGE

I. TOBY'S INTRODUCTION TO THE CIRCUS 1

II. TOBY RUNS AWAY FROM HOME 11

III. THE NIGHT RIDE 21

IV. THE FIRST DAY WITH THE CIRCUS 32

V. THE COUNTERFEIT TEN-CENT PIECE 44

VI. A TENDER-HEARTED SKELETON 56

VII. AN ACCIDENT AND ITS CONSEQUENCES 70

VIII. CAPTURE OF THE MONKEYS 81

IX. THE DINNER PARTY 90

X. MR. STUBBS AT A PARTY 106

XI. A STORMY NIGHT 119

XII. TOBY'S GREAT MISFORTUNE 131

XIII. TOBY ATTEMPTS TO RESIGN HIS SITUATION . . . 144

XIV. MR. CASTLE TEACHES TOBY TO RIDE 156

XV. TOBY'S FRIENDS PRESENT HIM WITH A COSTUME . 171

XVI. TOBY'S FIRST APPEARANCE IN THE RING 184

XVII. OFF FOR HOME! 197

XVIII. A DAY OF FREEDOM 215

XIX. MR. STUBBS'S MISCHIEF, AND HIS SAD FATE . . . 227

XX. HOME AND UNCLE DANIEL 240

TOBY TYLER

I

TOBY'S INTRODUCTION TO THE CIRCUS

"COULDN'T you give more 'n six peanuts for a cent?" was a question asked by a very small boy, with big, staring eyes, of a candy vender at a circus booth. And as he spoke he looked wistfully at the quantity of nuts piled high up on the basket, and then at the six, each of which now looked so small as he held them in his hand.

"Couldn't do it," was the reply of the proprietor of the booth, as he put the boy's penny carefully away in the drawer.

The little fellow looked for another moment at his purchase, and then carefully cracked the largest one.

A shade—and a very deep shade it was— of disappointment passed over his face, and then, looking up anxiously, he asked, "Don't you swap 'em when they're bad?"

The man's face looked as if a smile had been a stranger to it for a long time; but one did pay it a visit just then, and he tossed the boy two nuts, and asked him a question at the same time. "What is your name?"

The big brown eyes looked up for an instant, as if to learn whether the question was asked in good faith, and then their owner said, as he carefully picked apart another nut, "Toby Tyler."

"Well, that's a queer name."

"Yes, I s'pose so, myself; but, you see, I don't expect that's the name that belongs to me. But the fellers call me so, an' so does Uncle Dan'l."

"Who is Uncle Daniel?" was the next question. In the absence of other customers the man seemed disposed to get as much amusement out of the boy as possible.

"He hain't my uncle at all; I only call him so because all the boys do, an' I live with him."

"Where's your father and mother?"

"I don't know," said Toby, rather carelessly. "I don't know much about 'em, an'

2

Uncle Dan'l says they don't know much about me. Here's another bad nut; goin' to give me two more?"

The two nuts were given him, and he said, as he put them in his pocket and turned over and over again those which he held in his hand: "I shouldn't wonder if all of these was bad. S'posen you give me two for each one of 'em before I crack 'em, an' then they won't be spoiled so you can't sell 'em again."

As this offer of barter was made, the man looked amused, and he asked, as he counted out the number which Toby desired, "If I give you these, I suppose you'll want me to give you two more for each one, and you'll keep that kind of a trade going until you get my whole stock?"

"I won't open my head if every one of em's bad."

"All right; you can keep what you've got, and I'll give you these besides; but I don't want you to buy any more, for I don't want to do that kind of business."

Toby took the nuts offered, not in the least abashed, and seated himself on a convenient stone to eat them, and at the same time to see all that was going on around him. The coming of a circus to the little town of Guilford was an event, and Toby had hardly thought of anything else since the highly colored posters had first been put up. It was yet quite early in the morning, and the tents were just being erected by the men. Toby had followed, with eager eyes, everything that looked as if it belonged to the circus, from the time the first wagon had entered the town until the street parade had been made and everything was being prepared for the afternoon's performance.

The man who had made the losing trade in peanuts seemed disposed to question the boy still further, probably owing to the fact that he had nothing better to do.

"Who is this Uncle Daniel you say you live with? Is he a farmer?"

"No; he's a deacon, an' he raps me over the head with the hymn-book whenever I go to sleep in meetin', an' he says I eat four times as much as I earn. I blame him for hittin' so hard when I go to sleep, but I s'pose he's right about my eatin'. You see," and here his tone grew both confidential and mournful, "I am an awful eater, an' I can't seem to help it. Somehow I'm hungry all the time. I

4

don't seem ever to get enough till carrot time comes, an' then I can get all I want without troublin' anybody."

"Didn't you ever have enough to eat?"

"I s'pose I did; but you see Uncle Dan'l he found me one mornin' on his hay, an' he says I was cryin' for something to eat then, an' I've kept it up ever since. I tried to get him to give me money enough to go into the circus with; but he said a cent was all he could spare these hard times, an' I'd better take that an' buy something to eat with it, for the show wasn't very good, anyway. I wish peanuts wasn't but a cent a bushel."

"Then you would make yourself sick eating them."

"Yes, I s'pose I should; Uncle Dan'l says I'd eat till I was sick, if I got the chance; but I'd like to try it once."

He was a very small boy, with a round head covered with short red hair, a face as speckled as any turkey's egg, but thoroughly good-natured looking; and as he sat there on the rather sharp point of the rock, swaying his body to and fro as he hugged his knees with his hands, and kept his eyes fastened on the

5

tempting display of good things before him,
it would have been a very hard-hearted man
who would not have given him something.
But Mr. Job Lord, the proprietor of the booth,
was a hard-hearted man, and he did not make
the slightest advance toward offering the little
fellow anything.

Toby rocked himself silently for a moment,
and then he said, hesitatingly, "I don't
suppose you'd like to sell me some things,
an' let me pay you when I get older, would
you?"

Mr. Lord shook his head decidedly at this
proposition.

"I didn't s'pose you would," said Toby,
quickly; "but you didn't seem to be selling
anything, an' I thought I'd just see what
you'd say about it." And then he appeared
suddenly to see something wonderfully in-
teresting behind him, which served as an
excuse to turn his reddening face away.

"I suppose your uncle Daniel makes you
work for your living, don't he?" asked Mr.
Lord, after he had rearranged his stock of
candy and had added a couple of slices of
lemon peel to what was popularly supposed
to be lemonade.

6

"That's what I think; but he says that all
the work I do wouldn't pay for the meal that
one chicken would eat, an' I s'pose it's so,
for I don't like to work as well as a feller
without any father and mother ought to.
I don't know why it is, but I guess it's because
I take up so much time eatin' that it kinder
tires me out. I s'pose you go into the circus
whenever you want to, don't you?"

"Oh yes; I'm there at every performance,
for I keep the stand under the big canvas as
well as this one out here."

There was a great big sigh from out Toby's
little round stomach, as he thought what bliss
it must be to own all those good things and
to see the circus wherever it went. "It
must be nice," he said, as he faced the booth
and its hard-visaged proprietor once more.

"How would you like it?" asked Mr. Lord,
patronizingly, as he looked Toby over in a
business way, very much as if he contemplated
purchasing him.

"Like it!" echoed Toby. "Why, I'd grow
fat on it!"

"I don't know as that would be any ad-
vantage," continued Mr. Lord, reflectively,
"for it strikes me that you're about as fat

1   7

now as a boy of your age ought to be. But I've a great mind to give you a chance."

"What!" cried Toby, in amazement, and his eyes opened to their widest extent as this possible opportunity of leading a delightful life presented itself.

"Yes, I've a great mind to give you the chance. You see," and now it was Mr. Lord's turn to grow confidential, "I've had a boy with me this season, but he cleared out at the last town, and I'm running the business alone now."

Toby's face expressed all the contempt he felt for the boy who would run away from such a glorious life as Mr. Lord's assistant must lead; but he said not a word, waiting in breathless expectation for the offer which he now felt certain would be made him.

"Now I ain't hard on a boy," continued Mr. Lord, still confidentially, "and yet that one seemed to think that he was treated worse and made to work harder than any boy in the world."

"He ought to live with Uncle Dan'l a week," said Toby, eagerly.

"Here I was just like a father to him," said Mr. Lord, paying no attention to the

8

interruption, "and I gave him his board and lodging, and a dollar a week besides."

"Could he do what he wanted to with the dollar?"

"Of course he could. I never checked him, no matter how extravagant he was, an' yet I've seen him spend his whole week's wages at this very stand in one afternoon. And even after his money had all gone that way, I've paid for peppermint and ginger out of my own pocket just to cure his stomach-ache."

Toby shook his head mournfully, as if deploring that depravity which could cause a boy to run away from such a tender-hearted employer and from such a desirable position. But even as he shook his head so sadly he looked wistfully at the peanuts, and Mr. Lord observed the look.

It may have been that Mr. Job Lord was the tender-hearted man he prided himself upon being, or it may have been that he wished to purchase Toby's sympathy; but, at all events, he gave him a large handful of nuts, and Toby never bothered his little round head as to what motive prompted the gift. Now he could listen to the story of the boy's

9

treachery and eat at the same time; therefore he was an attentive listener.

"All in the world that boy had to do," continued Mr. Lord, in the same injured tone he had previously used, "was to help me set things to rights when we struck a town in the morning, and then tend to the counter till we left the town at night, and all the rest of the time he had to himself. Yet that boy was ungrateful enough to run away."

Mr. Lord paused, as if expecting some expression of sympathy from his listener; but Toby was so busily engaged with his unexpected feast, and his mouth was so full, that it did not seem even possible for him to shake his head.

"Now what should you say if I told you that you looked to me like a boy that was made especially to help run a candy counter at a circus, and if I offered the place to you?"

Toby made one frantic effort to swallow the very large mouthful, and in a choking voice he answered, quickly, "I should say I'd go with you, an' be mighty glad of the chance."

"Then it's a bargain, my boy, and you shall leave town with me to-night."

II

TOBY RUNS AWAY FROM HOME

TOBY could scarcely restrain himself at the prospect of this golden future that had so suddenly opened before him. He tried to express his gratitude, but could only do so by evincing his willingness to commence work at once.

"No, no, that won't do," said Mr. Lord, cautiously. "If your uncle Daniel should see you working here, he might mistrust something, and then you couldn't get away."

"I don't believe he'd try to stop me," said Toby, confidently; "for he's told me lots of times that it was a sorry day for him when he found me."

"We won't take any chances, my son," was the reply, in a very benevolent tone, as he patted Toby on the head and at the same time handed him a piece of pasteboard. "There's a ticket for the circus, and you come around to see me about ten o'clock to-night. I'll put you on one of the wagons, and by to-morrow morning your uncle Daniel will have hard work to find you."

If Toby had followed his inclinations, the chances are that he would have fallen on his knees and kissed Mr. Lord's hands in the excess of his gratitude. But not knowing exactly how such a show of thankfulness might be received, he contented himself by repeatedly promising that he would be punctual to the time and place appointed.

He would have loitered in the vicinity of the candy stand in order that he might gain some insight into the business; but Mr. Lord advised him to remain away, lest his uncle Daniel would see him, and suspect where he had gone when he was missed in the morning.

As Toby walked around the circus grounds, whereon was so much to attract his attention, he could not prevent himself from assuming an air of proprietorship. His interest in all that was going on was redoubled, and in his anxiety that everything should be done correctly and in the proper order he actually, and perhaps for the first time in his life, forgot that he was hungry. He was really to travel with a circus, to become a part, as it were, of the whole, and to be able to see its many wonderful and beautiful attractions every day.

Even the very tent ropes had acquired a new interest for him, and the faces of the men at work seemed suddenly to have become those of friends. How hard it was for him to walk around unconcernedly: and how especially hard to prevent his feet from straying toward that tempting display of dainties which he was to sell to those who came to see and enjoy, and who would look at him with wonder and curiosity! It was very hard not to be allowed to tell his playmates of his wonderfully good fortune; but silence meant success, and he locked his secret in his bosom, not even daring to talk with anyone he knew, lest he should betray himself by some incautious word.

He did not go home to dinner that day, and once or twice he felt impelled to walk past the candy stand, giving a mysterious shake of the head at the proprietor as he did so. The afternoon performance passed off as usual to all of the spectators save Toby. He imagined that each one of the performers knew that he was about to join them; and even as he passed the cage containing the monkeys he fancied that one particularly old one knew all about his intention of running away.

Of course it was necessary for him to go home at the close of the afternoon's performance, in order to get one or two valuable articles of his own—such as a boat, a kite, and a pair of skates—and in order that his actions might not seem suspicious. Before he left the grounds, however, he stole slyly around to the candy stand, and informed Mr. Job Lord, in a very hoarse whisper, that he would be on hand at the time appointed.

Mr. Lord patted him on the head, gave him two large sticks of candy, and, what was more kind and surprising, considering the fact that he wore glasses and was cross-eyed, he winked at Toby. A wink from Mr. Lord must have been intended to convey a great deal, because, owing to the defect in his eyes, it required no little exertion, and even then could not be considered as a really first-class wink.

That wink, distorted as it was, gladdened Toby's heart immensely and took away nearly all the sting of the scolding with which Uncle Daniel greeted him when he reached home.

That night—despite the fact that he was going to travel with the circus, despite the fact that his home was not a happy or cheerful one—Toby was not in a pleasant frame of mind. He began to feel for the first time that he was doing wrong; and as he gazed at Uncle Daniel's stern, forbidding-looking face, it seemed to have changed somewhat from its severity, and caused a great lump of something to come up in his throat as he thought that perhaps he should never see it again. Just then one or two kind words would have prevented him from running away, bright as the prospect of circus life appeared.

It was almost impossible for him to eat anything, and this very surprising state of affairs attracted the attention of Uncle Daniel.

"Bless my heart! what ails the boy?" asked the old man, as he peered over his glasses at Toby's well-filled plate, which was usually emptied so quickly. "Are ye sick, Toby, or what is the matter with ye?"

"No, I hain't sick," said Toby, with a sigh; "but I've been to the circus, an' I got a good deal to eat."

"Oho! You spent that cent I give ye, eh, an' got so much that it made ye sick?"

2

Toby thought of the six peanuts which he had bought with the penny Uncle Daniel had given him; and, amid all his homesickness, he could not help wondering if Uncle Daniel ever made himself sick with only six peanuts when he was a boy.

As no one paid any further attention to Toby, he pushed back his plate, arose from the table, and went with a heavy heart to attend to his regular evening chores. The cow, the hens, and even the pigs came in for a share of his unusually kind attention; and as he fed them all the big tears rolled down his cheeks as he thought that perhaps never again would he see any of them. These dumb animals had all been Toby's confidants; he had poured out his griefs in their ears, and fancied, when the world or Uncle Daniel had used him unusually hard, that they sympathized with him. Now he was leaving them forever, and as he locked the stable door he could hear the sounds of music coming from the direction of the circus grounds, and he was angry at it, because it represented that which was taking him away from his home, even though it was not as pleasant as it might have been.

Still, he had no thought of breaking the engagement which he had made. He went to his room, made a bundle of his worldly possessions, and crept out of the back door, down the road to the circus.

Mr. Lord saw him as soon as he arrived on the grounds, and as he passed another ticket to Toby he took his bundle from him, saying, as he did so: "I'll pack up your bundle with my things, and then you'll be sure not to lose it. Don't you want some candy?"

Toby shook his head; he had just discovered that there was possibly some connection between his heart and his stomach, for his grief at leaving home had taken from him all desire for good things. It is also more than possible that Mr. Lord had had experience enough with boys to know that they might be homesick on the eve of starting to travel with a circus; and in order to make sure that Toby would keep to his engagement he was unusually kind.

That evening was the longest Toby ever knew. He wandered from one cage of animals to another; then to see the performance in the ring, and back again to the animals, in the vain hope of passing the time pleasantly.

But it was of no use; that lump in his throat would remain there, and the thoughts of what he was about to do would trouble him severely. The performance failed to interest him, and the animals did not attract until he had visited the monkey cage for the third or fourth time. Then he fancied that the same venerable monkey who had looked so knowing in the afternoon was gazing at him with a sadness which could only have come from a thorough knowledge of all the grief and doubt that was in his heart.

There was no one around the cages, and Toby got just as near to the iron bars as possible. No sooner had he flattened his little pug nose against the iron than the aged monkey came down from the ring in which he had been swinging, and, seating himself directly in front of Toby's face, looked at him most compassionately.

It would not have surprised the boy just then if the animal had spoken; but as he did not, Toby did the next best thing and spoke to him.

"I s'pose you remember that you saw me this afternoon, an' somebody told you that I was goin' to join the circus, didn't they?"

The monkey made no reply, though Toby

fancied that he winked an affirmative answer; and he looked so sympathetic that he continued, confidentially:

"Well, I'm the same feller, an' I don't mind telling you that I'm awfully sorry that I promised that candy man I'd go with him. Do you know that I came near crying at the supper table to-night; an' Uncle Dan'l looked real good an' nice, though I never thought so before. I wish I wasn't goin', after all, 'cause it don't seem a bit like a good time now; but I s'pose I must, 'cause I promised to, an' 'cause the candy man has got all my things."

The big tears had begun to roll down Toby's cheeks, and as he ceased speaking the monkey reached out one little paw, which Toby took as earnestly as if it had been done purposely to console him.

"You're real good, you are," continued Toby; "an' I hope I shall see you real often, for it seems to me now, when there hain't any folks around, as if you was the only friend I've got in this great big world. It's awful when a feller feels the way I do, an' when he don't seem to want anything to eat. Now if you'll stick to me I'll stick to you, an' then it won't be half so bad when we feel this way."

During this speech Toby had still clung to the little brown paw, which the monkey now withdrew, and continued to gaze into the boy's face.

"The fellers all say I don't amount to anything," sobbed Toby, "an' Uncle Dan'l says I don't, an' I s'pose they know; but I tell you I feel just as bad, now that I'm goin' away from them all, as if I was as good as any of them."

At this moment Toby saw Mr. Lord enter the tent, and he knew that the summons to start was about to be given.

"Good-by," he said to the monkey, as he vainly tried to take him by the hand again. "Remember what I've told you, an' don't forget that Toby Tyler is feelin' worse to-night than if he was twice as big an' twice as good."

Mr. Lord had come to summon him away, and he now told Toby that he would show him with which man he was to ride that night.

Toby looked another good-by at the venerable monkey, who was watching him closely, and then followed his employer out of the tent, among the ropes and poles and general confusion attendant upon the removal of a circus from one place to another.

III

THE NIGHT RIDE

THE wagon on which Mr. Lord was to send his new-found employee was, by the most singular chance, the one containing the monkeys, and Toby accepted this as a good omen. He would be near his venerable friend all night, and there was some consolation in that. The driver instructed the boy to watch his movements, and when he saw him leading his horses around, "to look lively and be on hand, for he never waited for anyone."

Toby not only promised to do as ordered, but he followed the driver around so closely that, had he desired, he could not have rid himself of his little companion.

The scene which presented itself to Toby's view was strange and weird in the extreme. Shortly after he had attached himself to the man with whom he was to ride, the performance was over, and the work of putting the

show and its belongings into such a shape as
could be conveyed from one town to another
was soon in active operation. Toby forgot
his grief, forgot that he was running away
from the only home he had ever known—in
fact, forgot everything concerning himself—
so interested was he in that which was going
on about him.

As soon as the audience had got out of the
tent and almost before—the work of taking
down the canvas was begun.

Torches were stuck in the earth at regular
intervals, the lights that had shone so bril-
liantly in and around the ring had been ex-
tinguished, the canvas sides had been taken
off, and the boards that had formed the seats
were being packed into one of the carts with
a rattling sound that seemed as if a regular
fusillade of musketry was being indulged in.
Men were shouting; horses were being driven
hither and thither, harnessed to the wagons, or
drawing the huge carts away as soon as they
were loaded; and everything seemed in the
greatest state of confusion, while really the
work was being done in the most systematic
manner possible.

Toby had not long to wait before the driver

informed him that the time for starting had arrived, and assisted him to climb up to the narrow seat whereon he was to ride that night.

The scene was so exciting, and his efforts to stick to the narrow seat so great, that he really had no time to attend to the homesick feeling that had crept over him during the first part of the evening.

The long procession of carts and wagons drove slowly out of the town, and when the last familiar house had been passed the driver spoke to Toby for the first time, since they started.

"Pretty hard work to keep on—eh, sonny?"

"Yes," replied the boy, as the wagon jolted over a rock, bouncing him high in air, and he, by strenuous efforts, barely succeeded in alighting on the seat again, "it is pretty hard work; an' my name's Toby Tyler."

Toby heard a queer sound that seemed to come from the man's throat, and for a few moments he feared that his companion was choking. But he soon understood that this was simply an attempt to laugh, and he at once decided that it was a very poor style of laughing.

23

"So you object to being called sonny, do you?"

"Well, I'd rather be called Toby, for, you see, that's my name."

"All right, my boy; we'll call you Toby. I suppose you thought it was a mighty fine thing to run away an' jine a circus, didn't you?"

Toby started in affright, looked around cautiously, and then tried to peer down through the small square aperture, guarded by iron rods, that opened into the cage just back of the seat they were sitting on. Then he turned slowly around to the driver, and asked, in a voice sunk to a whisper: "How did you know that I was runnin' away? Did he tell you?" and Toby motioned with his thumb as if he were pointing out someone behind him.

It was the driver's turn now to look around in search of the "he" referred to by Toby.

"Who do you mean?" asked the man, impatiently.

"Why, the old feller; the one in the cart there. I think he knew I was runnin' away, though he didn't say anything about it; but he looked just as if he did."

24

The driver looked at Toby in perfect amazement for a moment, and then, as if suddenly understanding the boy, relapsed into one of those convulsive efforts that caused the blood to rush up into his face and gave him every appearance of having a fit.

"You must mean one of the monkeys," said the driver, after he had recovered his breath, which had been almost shaken out of his body by the silent laughter. "So you thought a monkey had told me what any fool could have seen if he had watched you for five minutes."

"Well," said Toby, slowly, as if he feared he might provoke one of those terrible laughing spells again, "I saw him to-night, an' he looked as if he knew what I was doin'; so I up an' told him, an' I didn't know but he'd told you, though he didn't look to me like a feller that would be mean."

There was another internal shaking on the part of the driver, which Toby did not fear so much, since he was getting accustomed to it, and then the man said, "Well, you are the queerest little cove I ever saw."

"I s'pose I am," was the reply, accompanied by a long-drawn sigh. "I don't seem to amount to so much as the other fellers do, an' I guess it's because I'm always hungry; you see, I eat awful, Uncle Dan'l says."

The only reply which the driver made to this plaintive confession was to put his hand down into the deepest recesses of one of his deep pockets and to draw therefrom a huge doughnut, which he handed to his companion.

Toby was so much at his ease by this time that the appetite which had failed him at supper had now returned in full force, and he devoured the doughnut in a most ravenous manner.

"You're too small to eat so fast," said the man, in a warning tone, as the last morsel of the greasy sweetness disappeared, and he fished up another for the boy. "Some time you'll get hold of one of the India-rubber doughnuts that they feed to circus people, an' choke yourself to death."

Toby shook his head, and devoured this second cake as quickly as he had the first, craning his neck, and uttering a funny little squeak as the last bit went down, just as a chicken does when he gets too large a mouthful of dough.

"I'll never choke," he said, confidently.

"I'm used to it; and Uncle Dan'l says I could eat a pair of boots an' never wink at 'em; but I don't just believe that."

As the driver made no reply to this remark Toby watched with no little interest all that was passing on around him. Each of the wagons had a lantern fastened to the hind axle, and these lights could be seen far ahead on the road, as if a party of fireflies had started in single file on an excursion. The trees by the side of the road stood out weird and ghostly looking in the darkness, and the rumble of the carts ahead and behind formed a musical accompaniment to the picture that sounded strangely doleful.

Mile after mile was passed over in perfect silence, save now and then when the driver would whistle a few bars of some very dismal tune that would fairly make Toby shiver with its mournfulness. Eighteen miles was the distance from Guilford to the town where the next performance of the circus was to be given, and as Toby thought of the ride before them it seemed as if the time would be almost interminable. He curled himself up on one corner of the seat, and tried very hard to go to sleep; but just as his eyes began to grow heavy the wagon would jolt over some rock or sink deep in some rut, till Toby, the breath very nearly shaken out of his body, and his neck almost dislocated, would sit bolt upright, clinging to the seat with both hands, as if he expected each moment to be pitched out into the mud.

The driver watched him closely, and each time that he saw him shaken up and awakened so thoroughly he would indulge in one of his silent laughing spells, until Toby would wonder whether he would ever recover from it. Several times had Toby been awakened, and each time he had seen the amusement his sufferings caused, until he finally resolved to put an end to the sport by keeping awake.

"What is your name?" he asked of the driver, thinking a conversation would be the best way to rouse himself into wakefulness.

"Waal," said the driver, as he gathered the reins carefully in one hand, and seemed to be debating in his mind how he should answer the question, "I don't know as I know myself, it's been so long since I've heard it."

Toby was wide enough awake now, as this rather singular problem was forced upon his mind. He revolved the matter silently for some moments, and at last he asked, "What do folks call you when they want to speak to you?"

"They always call me Old Ben, an' I've got so used to the name that I don't need any other."

Toby wanted very much to ask more questions, but he wisely concluded that it would not be agreeable to his companion.

"I'll ask the old man about it," said Toby to himself, referring to the aged monkey, whom he seemed to feel acquainted with; "he most likely knows, if he'll say anything." After this the conversation ceased, until Toby again ventured to suggest, "It's a pretty long drive, hain't it?"

"You want to wait till you've been in this business a year or two," said Ben, sagely, "an' then you won't think much of it. Why, I've known the show towns to be thirty miles apart, an' them was the times when we had lively work of it. Riding all night and working all day kind of wears on a fellow."

"Yes, I s'pose so," said Toby, with a sigh, as he wondered whether he had got to work as hard as that; "but I s'pose you get all you want to eat, don't you?"

"Now you've struck it!" said Ben, with the air of one about to impart a world of wisdom, as he crossed one leg over the other, that his position might be as comfortable as possible while he was initiating his young companion into the mysteries of the life. "I've had all the boys ride with me since I've been with this show, an' I've tried to start them right; but they didn't seem to profit by it, an' always got sick of the show an' run away, just because they didn't look out for themselves as they ought to. Now listen to me, Toby, an' remember what I say. You see they put us all in a hotel together, an' some of these places where we go don't have any too much stuff on the table. Whenever we strike a new town you find out at the hotel what time they have the grub ready, an' you be on hand, so's to get in with the first. Eat all you can, an' fill your pockets."

"If that's all a feller has to do to travel with a circus," said Toby, "I'm just the one, 'cause I always used to do just that when I hadn't any idea of bein' a circus man."

"Then you'll get along all right," said Ben, as he checked the speed of his horses and, looking carefully ahead, said, as he guided his team to one side of the road, "This is as far as we're going to-night."

Toby learned that they were within a couple of miles of the town, and that the entire procession would remain by the roadside until time to make the grand entrée into the village, when every wagon, horse, and man would be decked out in the most gorgeous array, as they had been when they entered Guilford.

Under Ben's direction he wrapped himself in an old horse blanket, and lay down on the top of the wagon; and he was so tired from the excitement of the day and night that he had hardly stretched out at full length before he was fast asleep.

3

IV

THE FIRST DAY WITH THE CIRCUS

WHEN Toby awakened and looked around he could hardly realize where he was or how he came there. As far ahead and behind on the road as he could see the carts were drawn up on one side; men were hurrying to and fro, orders were being shouted, and everything showed that the entry into the town was about to be made. Directly opposite the wagon on which he had been sleeping were the four elephants and two camels, and close behind, contentedly munching their breakfasts, were a number of tiny ponies. Troops of horses were being groomed and attended to; the road was littered with saddles, flags, and general decorations, until it seemed to Toby that there must have been a smash-up, and that he now beheld ruins rather than systematic disorder.

How different everything looked now, com-

pared to the time when the cavalcade marched
into Guilford, dazzling everyone with the gorgeous display! Then the horses pranced gayly
under their gaudy decorations, the wagons
were bright with glass, gilt, and flags, the
lumbering elephants and awkward camels
were covered with fancifully embroidered
velvets, and even the drivers of the wagons
were resplendent in their uniforms of scarlet
and gold. Now, in the gray light of the early
morning, everything was changed. The horses
were tired and muddy, and wore old and dirty
harness; the gilded chariots were covered with
mud-bespattered canvas, which caused them
to look like the most ordinary of market
wagons; the elephants and camels looked
dingy, dirty, almost repulsive; and the drivers
were only a sleepy-looking set of men, who,
in their shirt sleeves, were getting ready for
the change which would dazzle the eyes of
the inhabitants of the town.

Toby descended from his lofty bed, rubbed
his eyes to thoroughly awaken himself, and,
under the guidance of Ben, went to a little
brook near by and washed his face. He had
been with the circus not quite ten hours,
but now he could not realize that it had ever

seemed bright and beautiful. He missed his
comfortable bed, the quiet and cleanliness,
and the well-spread table; even although he
had felt the lack of parents' care, Uncle
Daniel's home seemed the very abode of love
and friendly feeling compared with this condition, where no one appeared to care even
enough for him to scold at him. He was
thoroughly homesick, and heartily wished
that he was back in his old native town.

While he was washing his face in the brook
he saw some of the boys who had come out
from the town to catch the first glimpse of
the circus, and he saw at once that he was
the object of their admiring gaze. He heard
one of the boys say, when they first discovered
him:

"There's one of them, an' he's only a little
feller; so I'm going to talk to him."

The evident admiration which the boys had
for Toby pleased him, and this pleasure was
the only drop of comfort he had had since he
started. He hoped they would come and
talk with him; and, that they might have the
opportunity, he was purposely slow in making
his toilet.

The boys approached him shyly, as if they

had their doubts whether he was made of the
same material as themselves, and when they
got quite near to him and satisfied themselves
that he was only washing his face in much
the same way that any well-regulated boy
would do, the one who had called attention
to him said, half timidly, "Hello!"

"Hello!" responded Toby, in a tone that
was meant to invite confidence.

"Do you belong to the circus?"

"Yes," said Toby, a little doubtfully.

Then the boys stared at him again as if he
were one of the strange-looking animals, and
the one who had been the spokesman drew
a long breath of envy as he said, longingly,
"My! what a nice time you must have!"

Toby remembered that only yesterday he
himself had thought that boys must have a
nice time with a circus, and he now felt what
a mistake that thought was; but he concluded that he would not undeceive his new
acquaintance.

"And do they give you frogs to eat, so's
to make you limber?"

This was the first time that Toby had
thought of breakfast, and the very mention
of eating made him hungry. He was just

at that moment so very hungry that he did not think he was replying to the question when he said, quickly: "Eat frogs! I could eat anything, if I only had the chance."

The boys took this as an answer to their question, and felt perfectly convinced that the agility of circus riders and tumblers depended upon the quantity of frogs eaten, and they looked upon Toby with no little degree of awe.

Toby might have undeceived them as to the kind of food he ate, but just at that moment the harsh voice of Mr. Job Lord was heard calling him, and he hurried away to commence his first day's work.

Toby's employer was not the same pleasant, kindly spoken man that he had been during the time they were in Guilford and before the boy was absolutely under his control. He looked cross, he acted cross, and it did not take the boy very long to find out that he was very cross.

He scolded Toby roundly, and launched more oaths at his defenseless head than Toby had ever heard in his life. He was angry that the boy had not been on hand to help him, and also that he had been obliged to hunt for him.

36

Toby tried to explain that he had no idea of what he was expected to do, and that he had been on the wagon to which he had been sent, only leaving it to wash his face; but the angry man grew still more furious.

"Went to wash your face, did yer? Want to set yourself up for a dandy, I suppose, and think that you must souse that speckled face of yours into every brook you come to? I'll soon break you of that; and the sooner you understand that I can't afford to have you wasting your time in washing the better it will be for you."

Toby now grew angry, and, not realizing how wholly he was in the man's power, he retorted: "If you think I'm going round with a dirty face, even if it is speckled, for a dollar a week, you're mistaken, that's all. How many folks would eat your candy if they knew you handled it over before you washed your hands?"

"Oho! I've picked up a preacher, have I? Now I want you to understand, my bantam, that I do all the preaching as well as the practicing myself, and this is about as quick a way as I know of to make you understand it."

37

As the man spoke he grasped the boy by the coat collar with one hand and with the other plied a thin rubber cane with no gentle force to every portion of Toby's body that he could reach.

Every blow caused the poor boy the most intense pain; but he determined that his tormentor should not have the satisfaction of forcing an outcry from him, and he closed his lips so tightly that not a single sound could escape from them.

This very silence enraged the man so much that he redoubled the force and rapidity of his blows, and it is impossible to say what might have been the consequences had not Ben come that way just then and changed the aspect of affairs.

"Up to your old tricks of whipping the boys, are you, Job?" he said, as he wrested the cane from the man's hand and held him off at arm's length, to prevent him from doing Toby more mischief.

Mr. Lord struggled to release himself, and insisted that, since the boy was in his employ, he should do with him just as he saw fit.

"Now look here, Mr. Lord," said Ben, as gravely as if he was delivering some profound piece of wisdom, "I've never interfered with you before; but now I'm going to stop your game of thrashing your boy every morning before breakfast. You just tell this youngster what you want him to do, and if he don't do it you can discharge him. If I hear of your flogging him, I shall attend to your case at once. You hear me?"

Ben shook the now terrified candy vender much as if he had been a child, and then released him, saying to Toby as he did so, "Now, my boy, you attend to your business as you ought to, and I'll settle his accounts if he tries the flogging game again."

"You see, I don't know what there is for me to do," sobbed Toby, for the kindly interference of Ben had made him show more feeling than Mr. Lord's blows had done.

"Tell him what he must do," said Ben, sternly.

"I want him to go to work and wash the tumblers, and fix up the things in that green box, so we can commence to sell as soon as we get into town," snarled Mr. Lord, as he motioned toward a large green chest that had been taken out of one of the carts, and which Toby saw was filled with dirty glasses, spoons,

39

knives, and other utensils such as were necessary to carry on the business.

Toby got a pail of water from the brook, hunted around and found towels and soap, and devoted himself to his work with such industry that Mr. Lord could not repress a grunt of satisfaction as he passed him, however angry he felt because he could not administer the whipping which would have smoothed his ruffled temper.

By the time the procession was ready to start for the town Toby had as much of his work done as he could find that it was necessary to do, and his master, in his surly way, half acknowledged that this last boy of his was better than any he had had before.

Although Toby had done his work so well he was far from feeling happy; he was both angry and sad as he thought of the cruel blows that had been inflicted, and he had plenty of leisure to repent of the rash step he had taken, although he could not see very clearly how he was to get away from it. He thought that he could not go back to Guilford, for Uncle Daniel would not allow him to come to his house again; and the hot scalding tears ran down his cheeks as he realized that he was homeless and friendless in this great big world.

It was while he was in this frame of mind that the procession, all gaudy with flags, streamers, and banners, entered the town. Under different circumstances this would have been a most delightful day for him, for the entrance of a circus into Guilford had always been a source of one day's solid enjoyment; but now he was the most disconsolate and unhappy boy in all that crowd.

He did not ride throughout the entire route of the procession, for Mr. Lord was anxious to begin business, and the moment the tenting ground was reached the wagon containing Mr. Lord's goods was driven into the inclosure and Toby's day's work began.

He was obliged to bring water, to cut up the lemons, fetch and carry fruit from the booth in the big tent to the booth on the outside, until he was ready to drop with fatigue, and, having had no time for breakfast, was nearly famished.

It was quite noon before he was permitted to go to the hotel for something to eat, and then Ben's advice to be one of the first to get to the tables was not needed.

In the eating line that day he astonished the servants, the members of the company, and even himself, and by the time he arose from the table, with both pockets and his stomach full to bursting, the tables had been set and cleared away twice while he was making one meal.

"Well, I guess you didn't hurry yourself much," said Mr. Lord, when Toby returned to the circus ground.

"Oh yes, I did," was Toby's innocent reply: "I ate just as fast as I could"; and a satisfied smile stole over the boy's face as he thought of the amount of solid food he had consumed.

The answer was not one which was calculated to make Mr. Lord feel any more agreeably disposed toward his new clerk, and he showed his ill temper very plainly as he said, "It must take a good deal to satisfy you."

"I s'pose it does," calmly replied Toby. "Sam Merrill used to say that I took after Aunt Olive and Uncle Dan'l; one ate a good while, an' the other ate awful fast."

Toby could not understand what it was that Mr. Lord said in reply, but he could understand that his employer was angry at somebody or something, and he tried unusually hard to please him. He talked to the boys who had gathered around, to induce them to buy, washed the glasses as fast as they were used, tried to keep off the flies, and in every way he could think of endeavored to please his master.

V

THE COUNTERFEIT TEN-CENT PIECE

WHEN the doors of the big tent were opened, and the people began to crowd in, just as Toby had seen them do at Guilford, Mr. Lord announced to his young clerk that it was time for him to go into the tent to work. Then it was that Toby learned for the first time that he had two masters instead of one, and this knowledge caused him no little uneasiness. If the other one was anything like Mr. Lord, his lot would be just twice as bad, and he began to wonder whether he could even stand it one day longer.

As the boy passed through the tent on his way to the candy stand, where he was really to enter upon the duties for which he had run away from home, he wanted to stop for a moment and speak with the old monkey who he thought had taken such an interest in him. But when he reached the cage in which

44

his friend was confined, there was such a crowd around it that it was impossible for him to get near enough to speak without being overheard.

This was such a disappointment to the little fellow that the big tears came into his eyes, and in another instant would have gone rolling down his cheeks if his aged friend had not chanced to look toward him. Toby fancied that the monkey looked at him in the most friendly way, and then he was certain that he winked one eye. Toby felt that there was no mistake about that wink, and it seemed as if it was intended to convey comfort to him in his troubles. He winked back at the monkey in the most emphatic and grave manner possible, and then went on his way, feeling wonderfully comforted.

The work inside the tent was far different and much harder than it was outside. He was obliged to carry around among the audience trays of candy, nuts, and lemonade for sale, and he was expected to cry aloud the description of that which he offered. The partner of Mr. Lord, who had charge of the stand inside the tent, showed himself to be neither better nor worse than Mr. Lord him-

self. When Toby first presented himself for
work he handed him a tray filled with glasses
of lemonade, and told him to go among the
audience, crying, "Here's your nice cold
lemonade, only five cents a glass!"

Toby started to do as he was bidden; but
when he tried to repeat the words in anything
like a loud tone of voice they stuck in his
throat, and he found it next to impossible
to utter a sound above a whisper. It seemed
to him that everyone in the audience was
looking only at him, and the very sound of
his own voice made him afraid.

He went entirely around the tent once
without making a sale, and when he returned
to the stand he was at once convinced that
one of his masters was quite as bad as the
other. This one—and he knew that his name
was Jacobs, for he heard someone call him
so—very kindly told him that he would break
every bone in his body if he didn't sell something, and Toby confidently believed that he
would carry out his threat.

It was with a very heavy heart that he
started around again in obedience to Mr.
Jacobs's angry command; but this time he
did manage to cry out, in a very thin and very

46

squeaky voice, the words which he had been told to repeat.

This time—perhaps owing to his pitiful and imploring look, certainly not because of the noise he made—he met with very good luck, and sold every glass of the mixture which Messrs. Lord and Jacobs called lemonade, and went back to the stand for more.

He certainly thought he had earned a word of praise, and fully expected it as he put the empty glasses and money on the stand in front of Mr. Jacobs. But, instead of the kind words, he was greeted with a volley of curses; and the reason for it was that he had taken in payment for two of the glasses a lead ten-cent piece. Mr. Jacobs, after scolding poor little Toby to his heart's content, vowed that the amount should be kept from his first week's wages, and then handed back the coin, with orders to give it to the first man who gave him money to change, under the penalty of a severe flogging if he failed to do so.

Poor Toby tried to explain matters by saying: "You see, I don't know anything about money; I never had more 'n a cent at a time, an' you mustn't expect me to get posted all at once."

"I'll post you with a stick if you do it again; an' it won't be well for you if you bring that ten-cent piece back here!"

Now Toby was very well aware that to pass the coin, knowing it to be bad, would be a crime, and he resolved to take the consequences of which Mr. Jacobs had intimated, if he could not find the one who had given him the counterfeit and persuade him to give him good money in its stead. He remembered very plainly where he had sold each glass of lemonade, and he retraced his steps, glancing at each face carefully as he passed. At last he was confident that he saw the man who had gotten him into such trouble, and he climbed up the board seats, saying, as he stood in front of him and held out the coin : "Mister, this money that you gave me is bad. Won't you give me another one for it?"

The man was a rough-looking party who had taken his girl to the circus, and who did not seem at all disposed to pay any heed to Toby's request. Therefore he repeated it, and this time more loudly.

"Get out the way!" said the man, angrily. "How can you expect me to see the show if you stand right in front of me?"

"You'll like it better," said Toby, earnestly, "if you give me another ten-cent piece."

"Get out an' don't bother me!" was the angry rejoinder; and the little fellow began to think that perhaps he would be obliged to "get out" without getting his money.

It was becoming a desperate case, for the man was growing angry very fast and if Toby did not succeed in getting good money for the bad, he would have to take the consequences of which Mr. Jacobs had spoken.

"Please, mister," he said, imploringly— for his heart began to grow very heavy, and he was fearing that he should not succeed— "won't you please give me the money back? You know you gave it to me, an' I'll have to pay it if you don't."

The boy's lip was quivering, and those around began to be interested in the affair, while several in the immediate vicinity gave vent to their indignation that a man should try to cheat a boy out of ten cents by giving him counterfeit money.

The man whom Toby was speaking to was about to dismiss him with an angry reply, when he saw that those about him were not only interested in the matter, but were evidently taking sides with the boy against him; and knowing well that he had given the counterfeit money, he took another coin from his pocket and, handing it to Toby, said, "I didn't give you the lead piece; but you're making such a fuss about it that here's ten cents to make you keep quiet."

"I'm sure you did give me the money," said Toby, as he took the extended coin, "an' I'm much obliged to you for takin' it back. I didn't want to tell you before, 'cause you'd thought I was beggin'; but if you hadn't given me this, I 'xpect I'd have got an awful whippin', for Mr. Jacobs said he'd fix me if I didn't get the money for it."

The man looked sheepish enough as he put the bad money in his pocket, and Toby's innocently told story caused such a feeling in his behalf among those who sat near that he not only disposed of his entire stock then and there, but received from one gentleman twenty-five cents for himself. He was both proud and happy as he returned to Mr. Jacobs with empty glasses, and with the money to refund the amount of loss which would have been caused by the counterfeit.

But the worthy partner of Mr. Lord's

candy business had no words of encouragement for the boy who was trying so hard to please.

"Let that make you keep your eyes open," he growled out, sulkily; "an' if you get caught in that trap again, you won't be let off so easy."

Poor little Toby! his heart seemed ready to break; but his few hours' previous experience had taugnt him that there was but one thing to do, and that was to work just as hard as possible, trusting to some good fortune to enable him to get out of the very disagreeable position in which he had voluntarily placed himself.

He took the basket of candy that Mr. Jacobs handed him, and trudged around the circle of seats, selling far more because of the pitifulness of his face than because of the excellence of his goods; and even this worked to his disadvantage. Mr. Jacobs was keen enough to see why his little clerk sold so many goods, and each time that he returned to the stand he said something to him in an angry tone, which had the effect of deepening the shadow on the boy's face and at the same time increasing trade.

By the time the performance was over Toby had in his pocket a dollar and twenty-five cents which had been given him for himself by some of the kind-hearted in the audience, and he kept his hand almost constantly upon it, for the money seemed to him like some kind friend who would help him out of his present difficulties.

After the audience had dispersed, Mr. Jacobs set Toby at work washing the glasses and clearing up generally, and then the boy started toward the other portion of the store —that watched over by Mr. Lord. Not a person save the watchmen was in the tent, and as Toby went toward the door he saw his friend the monkey sitting in one corner of the cage, and apparently watching his every movement.

It was as if he had suddenly seen one of the boys from home, and Toby, uttering an exclamation of delight, ran up to the cage and put his hand through the wires.

The monkey, in the gravest possible manner, took one of the fingers in his paw, and Toby shook hands with him very earnestly.

"I was sorry that I couldn't speak to you when I went in this noon," said Toby, as if making an apology; "but, you see, there were so many around here to see you that I couldn't get the chance. Did you see me wink at you?"

The monkey made no reply, but he twisted his face into such a funny little grimace that Toby was quite as well satisfied as if he had spoken.

"I wonder if you hain't some relation to Steve Stubbs?" Toby continued, earnestly, "for you look just like him, only he don't have quite so many whiskers. What I wanted to say was that I'm awful sorry I run away. I used to think that Uncle Dan'l was bad enough; but he was just a perfect good Samarathon to what Mr. Lord an' Mr. Jacobs are; an' when Mr. Lord looks at me with that crooked eye of his I feel it 'way down in my boots. Do you know" and here Toby put his mouth nearer to the monkey's head and whispered—"I'd run away from this circus if I could get the chance. Wouldn't you?"

Just at this point, as if in answer to the question, the monkey stood up on his hind feet and reached out his paw to the boy, who seemed to think this was his way of being more emphatic in saying "Yes."

Toby took the paw in his hand, shook it again earnestly, and said, as he released it: "I was pretty sure you felt just about the same way I did, Mr. Stubbs, when I passed you this noon. Look here"—and Toby took the money from his pocket which had been given him—"I got all that this afternoon, an' I'll try an' stick it out somehow till I get as much as ten dollars, an' then we'll run away some night, an' go 'way off as far as—as—as out West; an' we'll stay there, too."

The monkey, probably tired with remaining in one position so long, started toward the top of the cage, chattering and screaming, joining the other monkeys, who had gathered in a little group in one of the swings.

"Now see here, Mr. Stubbs," said Toby, in alarm, "you mustn't go to telling everybody about it, or Mr. Lord will know, an' then we'll be dished, sure."

The monkey sat quietly in the swing, as if he felt reproved by what the boy had said; and Toby, considerably relieved by his silence, said, as he started toward the door, "That's right—mum's the word; you keep quiet, an' so will I, an' pretty soon we'll get away from the whole crowd."

54

All the monkeys chattered; and Toby, believing that everything which he had said had been understood by the animals, went out of the door to meet his other taskmaster.

VI

A TENDER-HEARTED SKELETON

"NOW, then, lazybones," was Mr. Lord's warning cry as Toby came out of the tent, "if you've fooled away enough of your time, you can come here an' tend shop for me while I go to supper. You crammed yourself this noon, an' it 'll teach you a good lesson to make you go without anything to eat to-night; it 'll make you move round more lively in future."

Instead of becoming accustomed to such treatment as he was receiving from his employers, Toby's heart grew more tender with each brutal word, and this last punishment—that of losing his supper—caused the poor boy more sorrow than blows would. Mr. Lord started for the hotel as he concluded his cruel speech; and poor little Toby, going behind the counter, leaned his head upon the rough boards and cried as if his heart would break.

All the fancied brightness and pleasure of a circus life had vanished, and in its place was the bitterness of remorse that he had repaid Uncle Daniel's kindness by the ingratitude of running away. Toby thought that if he could only nestle his little red head on the pillows of his little bed in that rough room at Uncle Daniel's, he would be the happiest and best boy, in the future, in all the great wide world.

While he was still sobbing away at a most furious rate he heard a voice close at his elbow, and, looking up, saw the thinnest man he had ever seen in all his life. The man had flesh-colored tights on, and a spangled red velvet garment—that was neither pants, because there were no legs to it, nor a coat, because it did not come above his waist— made up the remainder of his costume. Because he was so wonderfully thin, because of the costume which he wore, and because of a highly colored painting which was hanging in front of one of the small tents, Toby knew that the Living Skeleton was before him, and his big brown eyes opened all the wider as he gazed at him.

"What is the matter, little fellow?" asked the man, in a kindly tone. "What makes you

cry so? Has Job been up to his old tricks
again?"

"I don't know what his old tricks are"—
and Toby sobbed, the tears coming again
because of the sympathy which this man's
voice expressed for him—"but I know that
he's a mean, ugly thing—that's what I know;
an' if I could only get back to Uncle Dan'l,
there hain't elephants enough in all the
circuses in the world to pull me away
again."

"Oh, you run away from home, did you?"

"Yes, I did," sobbed Toby, "an' there
hain't any boy in any Sunday-school book
that ever I read that was half so sorry he'd
been bad as I am. It's awful; an' now I
can't have any supper, 'cause I stopped to
talk with Mr. Stubbs."

"Is Mr. Stubbs one of your friends?"
asked the skeleton, as he seated himself in
Mr. Lord's own private chair.

"Yes, he is, an' he's the only one in this
whole circus who 'pears to be sorry for me.
You'd better not let Mr. Lord see you sittin'
in that chair or he'll raise a row."

"Job won't raise any row with me," said
the skeleton. "But who is this Mr. Stubbs?

58

I don't seem to know anybody by that name."

"I don't think that is his name. I only call him so, 'cause he looks so much like a feller I know who is named Stubbs."

This satisfied the skeleton that this Mr. Stubbs must be someone attached to the show, and he asked:

"Has Job been whipping you?"

"No; Ben, the driver on the wagon where I ride, told him not to do that again; but he hain't going to let me have any supper, 'cause I was so slow about my work—though I wasn't slow; I only talked to Mr. Stubbs when there wasn't anybody round his cage."

"Sam! Sam! Sam-u-el!"

This name, which was shouted twice in a quick, loud voice, and the third time in a slow manner, ending almost in a screech, did not come from either Toby or the skeleton, but from an enormously large woman, dressed in a gaudy red-and-black dress, cut very short, and with low neck and an apology for sleeves, who had just come out from the tent whereon the picture of the Living Skeleton hung.

"Samuel," she screamed again, "come inside this minute, or you'll catch your

death o' cold, an' I shall have you wheezin'
around with the phthisic all night. Come
in, Sam-u-el."

"That's her," said the skeleton to Toby,
as he pointed his thumb in the direction of
the fat woman, but paying no attention
to the outcry she was making—"that's my
wife Lilly, an' she's the Fat Woman of the
show. She's always yellin' after me that way
the minute I get out for a little fresh air, an'
she's always sayin' just the same thing.
Bless you, I never have the phthisic, but she
does awful; an I s'pose 'cause she's so large
she can't feel all over her, an' thinks it's
me that has it."

"Is—is all that—is that your wife?" stammered Toby, in astonishment, as he looked at
the enormously fat woman who stood in the
tent door, and then at the wonderfully thin
man who sat beside him.

"Yes, that's her," said the skeleton. "She
weighs pretty nigh four hundred, though of
course the show cards says it's over six hundred, an' she earns almost as much money as I
do. Of course she can't get so much, for skele-
tons is much scarcer than fat folks; but we
make a pretty good thing travelin' together."

"Sam-u-el!" again came the cry from the fat woman, "are you never coming in?"

"Not yet, my angel," said the skeleton, placidly, as he crossed one thin leg over the other and looked calmly at her. "Come here an' see Job's new boy."

"Your imprudence is wearin' me away so that I sha'n't be worth five dollars a week to any circus," she said, impatiently, at the same time coming toward the candy stand quite as rapidly as her very great size would admit.

"This is my wife Lilly—Mrs. Treat," said the skeleton, with a proud wave of his hand, as he rose from his seat and gazed admiringly at her. "This is my flower—my queen, Mr.— Mr.—"

"Tyler," said Toby, supplying the name which the skeleton—or Mr. Treat, as Toby now learned his name was—did not know; "Tyler is my name—Toby Tyler."

"Why, what a little chap you are!" said Mrs. Treat, paying no attention to the awkward little bend of the head which Toby intended for a bow. "How small he is, Samuel!"

"Yes," said the skeleton, reflectively, as he

looked Toby over from head to foot, as if he were mentally trying to calculate exactly how many inches high he was, "he is small; but he's got all the world before him to grow in, an' if he only eats enough— There, that reminds me. Job isn't going to give him any supper, because he didn't work hard enough."

"He won't, won't he?" exclaimed the large lady, savagely. "Oh, he's a precious one, he is! An' some day I shall just give him a good shakin'-up, that's what I'll do. I get all out of patience with that man's ugliness."

"An' she'll do just what she says," said the skeleton to Toby, with an admiring shake of the head. "That woman hain't afraid of anybody, an' I wouldn't be a bit surprised if she did give Job a pretty rough time."

Toby thought, as he looked at her, that she was large enough to give 'most anyone a pretty rough time, but he did not venture to say so. While he was looking first at her, and then at her very thin husband, the skeleton told his wife the little that he had learned regarding the boy's history; and when he had concluded she waddled away toward her tent.

"Great woman that," said the skeleton, as he saw her disappear within the tent.

"Yes," said Toby, "she's the greatest I ever saw."

"I mean that she's got a great head. Now you'll see about how much she cares for what Job says."

"If I was as big as her," said Toby, with just a shade of envy in his voice, "I wouldn't be afraid of anybody."

"It hain't so much the size," said the skeleton, sagely—"it hain't so much the size, my boy; for I can scare that woman almost to death when I feel like it."

Toby looked for a moment at Mr. Treat's thin legs and arms, and then he said, warningly, "I wouldn't feel like it very often if I was you, Mr. Treat, 'cause she might break some of your bones if you didn't happen to scare her enough."

"Don't fear for me, my boy—don't fear for me; you'll see how I manage her if you stay with the circus long enough. Now I often—"

If Mr. Treat was about to confide a family secret to Toby, it was fated that he should not hear it then, for Mrs. Treat had just come out of her tent, carrying in her hands a large tin plate piled high with a miscellaneous assortment of pie, cake, bread, and meat.

She placed this in front of Toby, and as she did so she handed him two pictures.

"There, little Toby Tyler," she said— "there's something for you to eat, if Mr. Job Lord and his precious partner Jacobs did say you shouldn't have any supper; an' I've brought you a picture of Samuel an' me. We sell 'em for ten cents apiece, but I'm going to give them to you, because I like the looks of you."

Toby was quite overcome with the presents, and seemed at a loss how to thank her for them. He attempted to speak, but could not get the words out at first; and then he said, as he put the two photographs in the same pocket with his money: "You're awful good to me, an' when I get to be a man I'll give you lots of things. I wasn't so very hungry, if I am such a big eater, but I did want something."

"Bless your dear little heart, and you *shall* have something to eat," said the Fat Woman, as she seized Toby, squeezed him close up to her, and kissed his freckled face as kindly as if it had been as fair and white as possible. "You shall eat all you want to; an' if you get the stomach-ache, as Samuel does sometimes when he's been eatin' too much, I'll give

you some catnip tea out of the same dipper
that I give him his. He's a great eater,
Samuel is," she added, in a burst of confidence,
"an' it's a wonder to me what he does with
it all sometimes."

"Is he?" exclaimed Toby, quickly. "How
funny that is! for I'm an awful eater. Why,
Uncle Dan'l used to say that I ate twice as
much as I ought to, an' it never made me any
bigger. I wonder what's the reason?"

"I declare I don't know," said the Fat
Woman, thoughtfully, "an' I've wondered
at it time an' time again. Some folks is made
that way, an' some folks is made different.
Now I don't eat enough to keep a chicken
alive, an' yet I grow fatter an' fatter every
day—don't I, Samuel?"

"Indeed you do, my love," said the skeleton, with a world of pride in his voice; "but
you mustn't feel bad about it, for every pound
you gain makes you worth just so much
more to the show."

"Oh, I wasn't worryin', I was only won-
derin'. But we must go, Samuel, for the poor
child won't eat a bit while we are here. After
you've eaten what there is there, bring the
plate in to me," she said to Toby, as she took

her lean husband by the arm and walked him off toward their own tent.

Toby gazed after them a moment, and then he commenced a vigorous attack upon the eatables which had been so kindly given him. Of the food which he had taken from the dinner table he had eaten some while he was in the tent, and after that he had entirely forgotten that he had any in his pocket; therefore, at the time that Mrs. Treat had brought him such a liberal supply he was really very hungry.

He succeeded in eating nearly all the food which had been brought to him, and the very small quantity which remained he readily found room for in his pockets. Then he washed the plate nicely; and seeing no one in sight, he thought he could leave the booth long enough to return the plate.

He ran with it quickly into the tent occupied by the thin man and fat woman, and handed it to her, with a profusion of thanks for her kindness.

"Did you eat it all?" she asked.

"Well," hesitated Toby, "there was two doughnuts an' a piece of pie left over, an' I put them in my pocket. If you don't care, I'll eat them some time to-night."

"You shall eat it whenever you want to; an' any time that you get hungry again you come right to me."

"Thank you, marm. I must go now, for I left the store all alone."

"Run, then; an' if Job abuses you, just let me know it, an' I'll keep him from cuttin' up any monkeyshines."

Toby hardly heard the end of her sentence, so great was his haste to get back to the booth; and just as he emerged from the tent, on a quick run, he received a blow on the ear which sent him sprawling in the dust, and he heard Mr. Job Lord's angry voice as it said, "So, just the moment my back is turned you leave the stand to take care of itself, do you, an' run around tryin' to plot some mischief against me, eh?" And the brute kicked the prostrate boy twice with his heavy boot.

"Please don't kick me again!" pleaded Toby. "I wasn't gone but a minute, an' I wasn't doing anything bad."

"You're lying now, an' you know it, you young cub!" exclaimed the angry man as he advanced to kick the boy again. "I'll let you know who you've got to deal with when you get hold of me!"

"And I'll let you know who you've got to deal with when you get hold of me!" said a woman's voice; and just as Mr. Lord raised his foot to kick the boy again the fat woman seized him by the collar, jerked him back over one of the tent ropes, and left him quite as prostrate as he had left Toby. "Now, Job Lord," said the angry woman, as she towered above the thoroughly enraged but thoroughly frightened man, "I want you to understand that you can't knock and beat this boy while I'm around. I've seen enough of your capers, an' I'm going to put a stop to them. That boy wasn't in this tent more than two minutes, an' he attends to his work better than anyone you have ever had; so see that you treat him decent. Get up," she said to Toby, who had not dared to rise from the ground; "and if he offers to strike you again, come to me."

Toby scrambled to his feet, and ran to the booth in time to attend to one or two customers who had just come up. He could see from out the corner of his eye that Mr. Lord had arisen to his feet also, and was engaged in an angry conversation with Mrs. Treat, the result of which he very much feared would be another and a worse whipping for him.

But in this he was mistaken, for Mr. Lord, after the conversation was ended, came toward the booth, and began to attend to his business without speaking one word to Toby. When Mr. Jacobs returned from his supper, Mr. Lord took him by the arm and walked him out toward the rear of the tents; and Tony was very positive that he was to be the subject of their conversation, which made him not a little uneasy.

It was not until nearly time for the performance to begin that Mr. Lord returned, and he had nothing to say to Toby save to tell him to go into the tent and begin his work there. The boy was only too glad to escape so easily, and he went to his work with as much alacrity as if he were about entering upon some pleasure.

When he met Mr. Jacobs that gentleman spoke to him very sharply about being late, and seemed to think it no excuse at all that he had just been relieved from the outside work by Mr. Lord.

VII

AN ACCIDENT AND ITS CONSEQUENCES

TOBY'S experience in the evening was very similar to that of the afternoon, save that he was so fortunate as not to take any more bad money in payment for his goods. Mr. Jacobs scolded and swore alternately, and the boy really surprised him by his way of selling goods, though he was very careful not to say anything about it, but made Toby believe that he was doing only about half as much work as he ought to do. Toby's private hoard of money was increased that evening, by presents, ninety cents, and he began to look upon himself as almost a rich man.

When the performance was nearly over Mr. Jacobs called to him to help in packing up; and by the time the last spectator had left the tent the worldly possessions of Messrs. Lord and Jacobs were ready for removal, and Toby allowed to do as he had a mind to, so

long as he was careful to be on hand when
Old Ben was ready to start.

Toby thought that he would have time
to pay a visit to his friends the skeleton and
the Fat Woman, and to that end started
toward the place where their tent had been
standing; but to his sorrow he found that it
was already being taken down, and he had only
time to thank Mrs. Treat and to press the
fleshless hand of her shadowy husband as they
entered their wagon to drive away.

He was disappointed, for he had hoped to
be able to speak with his new-made friends
a few moments before the weary night's ride
commenced; but, failing in that, he went
hastily back to the monkeys' cage. Old Ben
was there, getting things ready for a start;
but the wooden sides of the cage had not
been put up, and Toby had no difficulty in
calling the aged monkey up to the bars. He
held one of the Fat Woman's doughnuts in
his hand, and said, as he passed it through to
the animal:

"I thought perhaps you might be hungry,
Mr. Stubbs, and this is some of what the
skeleton's wife gave me. I hain't got very
much time to talk with you now; but the

first chance I can get away to-morrow, an'
when there hain't anybody round, I want to
tell you something."

The monkey had taken the doughnut in
his handlike paws, and was tearing it to
pieces, eating small portions of it very rapidly.

"Don't hurry yourself," said Toby, warningly, "for Uncle Dan'l always told me the
worst thing a feller could do was to eat fast.
If you want any more, after we start, just
put your hand through the little hole up
there near the seat, an' I'll give you all you
want."

From the look on his face Toby confidently
believed the monkey was about to make some
reply; but just then Ben shut up the sides,
separating Toby and Mr. Stubbs, and the
order was given to start.

Toby clambered up on to the high seat, Ben
followed him, and in another instant the team
was moving along slowly down the dusty
road, preceded and followed by the many
wagons, with their tiny swinging lights.

"Well," said Ben, when he had got his team
well under way and felt that he could indulge
in a little conversation, "how did you get
along to-day?"

Toby related all of his movements, and gave the driver a faithful account of all that had happened to him, concluding his story by saying, "That was one of Mrs. Treat's doughnuts that I just gave to Mr. Stubbs."

"To whom?" asked Ben, in surprise.

"To Mr. Stubbs—the old fellow here in the cart, you know, that's been so good to me."

Toby heard a sort of gurgling sound, saw the driver's body sway back and forth in a trembling way, and was just becoming thoroughly alarmed, when he thought of the previous night, and understood that Ben was only laughing in his own peculiar way.

"How did you know his name was Stubbs?" asked Ben, after he had recovered his breath.

"Oh, I don't know that that is his real name," was the quick reply; "I only call him that because he looks so much like a feller with that name that I knew at home. He don't seem to mind because I call him Stubbs."

Ben looked at Toby earnestly for a moment, acting all the time as if he wanted to laugh again, but didn't dare to, for fear he might burst a blood vessel; and then he said, as he patted him on the shoulder: "Well, you are the queerest little fish that I ever saw in all

my travels. You seem to think that that
monkey knows all you say to him."

"I'm sure he does," said Toby, positively.
"He don't say anything right out to me, but
he knows everything I tell him. Do you
suppose he could talk if he tried to?"

"Look here, Mr. Toby Tyler"—and Ben
turned half around in his seat and looked Toby
full in the face, so as to give more emphasis
to his words—"are you heathen enough to
think that that monkey could talk if he
wanted to?"

"I know I hain't a heathen," said Toby,
thoughtfully, "for if I had been some of the
missionaries would have found me out a good
while ago; but I never saw anybody like
this old Mr. Stubbs before, an' I thought he
could talk if he wanted to, just as the Living
Skeleton does, or his wife. Anyhow, Mr.
Stubbs winked at me; an' how could he do
that if he didn't know what I've been sayin'
to him?"

"Look here, my son," said Ben, in a most
fatherly fashion, "monkeys hain't anything
but beasts, an' they don't know how to talk
any more than they know what you say to
'em."

"Didn't you ever hear any of them speak a word?"

"Never. I've been in a circus, man an' boy, nigh on to forty years, an' I never seen nothin' in a monkey more 'n any other beast, except their awful mischiefness."

"Well," said Toby, still unconvinced, "I believe Mr. Stubbs knows what I say to him, anyway."

"Now don't be foolish, Toby," pleaded Ben. "You can't show me one thing that a monkey ever did because you told him to."

Just at this moment Toby felt someone pulling at the back of his coat, and, looking round, he saw it was a little brown hand, reaching through the bars of the air hole of the cage, that was tugging away at his coat.

"There!" he said, triumphantly, to Ben. "Look there! I told Mr. Stubbs if he wanted anything more to eat, to tell me an' I would give it to him. Now you can see for yourself that he's come for it." And Toby took a doughnut from his pocket and put it into the tiny hand, which was immediately withdrawn. "Now what do you think of Mr. Stubbs knowing what I say to him?"

"They often stick their paws up through

75

there," said Ben, in a matter-of-fact tone. "I've had 'em pull my coat in the night till they made me as nervous as ever any old woman was. You see, Toby my boy, monkeys is monkeys; an' you mustn't go to gettin' the idea that they're anything else, for it's a mistake. You think this old monkey in here knows what you say? Why, that's just the cuteness of the old fellow—he watches you to see if he can't do just as you do, an' that's all there is about it."

Toby was more than half convinced that Ben was putting the matter in its proper light, and he would have believed all that had been said if, just at that moment, he had not seen that brown hand reaching through the hole to clutch him again by the coat.

The action seemed so natural, so like a hungry boy who gropes in the dark pantry for something to eat, that it would have taken more arguments than Ben had at his disposal to persuade Toby that his Mr. Stubbs could not understand all that was said to him. Toby put another doughnut in the outstretched hand, and then sat silently, as if in a brown study over some difficult problem.

For some time the ride was continued in

silence. Ben was going through all the motions of whistling without uttering a sound—a favorite amusement of his—and Toby's thoughts were far away in the humble home he had scorned, with Uncle Daniel, whose virtues had increased in his esteem with every mile of distance which had been put between them, and whose faults had decreased in a corresponding ratio.

Toby's thoughtfulness had made him sleepy, and his eyes were almost closed in slumber, when he was startled by a crashing sound, was conscious of a feeling of being hurled from his seat by some great force, and then he lay senseless by the side of the road, while the wagon became a perfect wreck, from out of which a small army of monkeys was escaping. Ben's experienced ear had told him at the first crash that his wagon was breaking down, and, without having time to warn Toby of his peril, he had leaped clear of the wreck, keeping his horses under perfect control and thus averting more trouble. It was the breaking of one of the axles which Toby had heard just before he was thrown from his seat and when the body of the wagon came down upon the hard road.

The monkeys, thus suddenly released from confinement, had scampered off in every direction, and by a singular chance Toby's aged friend started for the woods in such a direction as to bring him directly before the boy's insensible form. The monkey, on coming up to Toby, stopped, urged by the well-known curiosity of its race, and began to examine the boy's person carefully, prying into pockets and trying to open the boy's half-closed eyelids. Fortunately for Toby, he had fallen upon a mud bank and was only stunned for the moment, having received no serious bruises. The attentions bestowed upon him by the monkey served the purpose of bringing him to his senses; and, after he had looked around him in the gray light of the coming morning, it would have taken far more of a philosopher than Old Ben was to persuade the boy that monkeys did not possess reasoning faculties.

The monkey was busy at Toby's ears, nose, and mouth, as monkeys will do when they get an opportunity, and the expression of its face was as grave as possible. Toby firmly believed that the monkey's face showed sorrow at his fall, and he imagined that the attentions which were bestowed upon him were for the purpose of learning whether he had been injured or not.

"Don't worry, Mr. Stubbs," said Toby, anxious to reassure his friend, as he sat upright and looked about him. "I didn't get hurt any; but I would like to know how I got 'way over here."

It really seemed as if the monkey was pleased to know that his little friend was not hurt, for he seated himself on his haunches, and his face expressed the liveliest pleasure that Toby was well again—or at least that was how the boy interpreted the look.

By this time the news of the accident had been shouted ahead from one team to the other, and all hands were hurrying to the scene for the purpose of rendering aid. As Toby saw them coming he also saw a number of small forms, looking something like diminutive men, hurrying past him, and for the first time he understood how it was that the aged monkey was at liberty, and knew that those little dusky forms were the other occupants of the cage escaping to the woods.

"See there, Mr. Stubbs! see there!" he exclaimed, pointing toward the fugitives;

"they're all going off into the woods! What shall we do?"

The sight of the runaways seemed to excite the old monkey quite as much as it did the boy. He sprang to his feet, chattering in the most excited way, screamed two or three times, as if he were calling them back, and then started off in vigorous pursuit.

"Now he's gone too!" said Toby, disconsolately, believing the old fellow had run away from him. "I didn't think Mr. Stubbs would treat me this way!"

VIII

CAPTURE OF THE MONKEYS

THE boy tried to rise to his feet, but his head whirled so, and he felt so dizzy and sick from the effects of his fall, that he was obliged to sit down again until he should feel able to stand. Meanwhile the crowd around the wagon paid no attention to him, and he lay there quietly enough, until he heard the hateful voice of Mr. Lord asking if his boy were hurt.

The sound of his voice affected Toby very much as the chills and fever affect a sufferer, and he shook so with fear, and his heart beat so loudly, that he thought Mr. Lord must know where he was by the sound. Seeing, however, that his employer did not come directly toward him, the thought flashed upon his mind that now would be a good chance to run away, and he acted upon it at once. He rolled himself over in the mud until he reached a low growth of fir trees that skirted the road, and when beneath their friendly shade he rose to his feet and walked swiftly toward the woods, following the direction the monkeys had taken.

He no longer felt dizzy and sick; the fear of Mr. Lord had dispelled all that, and he felt strong and active again.

He had walked rapidly for some distance, and was nearly beyond the sound of the voices in the road, when he was startled by seeing quite a procession of figures emerge from the trees and come directly toward him.

He could not understand the meaning of this strange company, and it so frightened him that he attempted to hide behind a tree, in the hope that they might pass without seeing him. But no sooner had he secreted himself than a strange, shrill chattering came from the foremost of the group, and in an instant Toby emerged from his place of concealment.

He had recognized the peculiar sound as that of the old monkey who had left him a few moments before, and he knew now what he did not know then, owing to the darkness. The newcomers were the monkeys that had escaped from the cage, and had been overtaken and compelled to come back by the old monkey, who seemed to have the most perfect control over them.

The old fellow was leading the band, and all were linked "hand in hand" with each other, which gave the whole crowd a most comical appearance as they came up to Toby, half hopping, half walking upright, and all chattering and screaming, like a crowd of children out for a holiday.

Toby stepped toward the noisy crowd, held out his hand gravely to the old monkey, and said, in tones of heartfelt sorrow:

"I felt awful bad because I thought you had gone off an' left me, when you went off to find the other fellows. You're awful good, Mr. Stubbs; an' now, instead of runnin' away, as I was goin' to do, we'll all go back together."

The old monkey grasped Toby's extended hand with his disengaged paw, and, clinging firmly to it, the whole crowd followed in unbroken line, chattering and scolding at the most furious rate, while every now and then Mr. Stubbs would look back and scream out something, which would cause the confusion to cease for an instant.

It was really a comical sight, but Toby

seemed to think it the most natural thing in the world that they should follow him in this manner, and he chattered to the old monkey quite as fast as any of the others were doing. He told him very gravely all that he knew about the accident, explained why it was that he conceived the idea of running away, and really believed that Mr. Stubbs understood every word he was saying.

Very shortly after Toby had started to run away the proprietor of the circus drove up to the scene of disaster, and, after seeing that the wagon was being rapidly fixed up so that it could be hauled to the next town, he ordered that search should be made for the monkeys. It was very important that they should be captured at once, and he appeared to think more of the loss of the animals than of the damage done to the wagon.

While the men were forming a plan for a search for the truants, so that in case of a capture they could let one another know, the noise made by Toby and his party was heard, and the men stood still to learn what it meant.

The entire party burst into shouts of laughter as Toby and his companions walked into the circle of light formed by the glare of the lanterns, and the merriment was by no means abated at Toby's serious demeanor. The wagon was now standing upright, with the door open, and Toby therefore led his companions directly to it, gravely motioning them to enter.

The old monkey, instead of obeying, stepped back to Toby's side, and screamed to the others in such a manner that they all entered the cage, leaving him on the outside with the boy.

Toby motioned him to get in, too, but he clung to his hand, and scolded so furiously that it was apparent he had no idea of leaving his boy companion. One of the men stepped up and was about to force him into the wagon, when the proprietor ordered him to stop.

"What boy is that?" he asked.

"Job Lord's new boy," said someone in the crowd.

The man asked Toby how it was that he had succeeded in capturing all the runaways; and he answered, gravely:

"Mr. Stubbs an' I are good friends, an' when he saw the others runnin' away he just stopped 'em an' brought 'em back to me.

7 85

I wish you'd let Mr. Stubbs ride with me; we like each other a good deal."

"You can do just what you please with Mr. Stubbs, as you call him. I expected to lose half the monkeys in that cage, and you have brought back every one. That monkey shall be yours, and you may put him in the cage whenever you want to, or take him with you, just as you choose, for he belongs entirely to you."

Toby's joy knew no bounds; he put his arm around the monkey's neck, and the monkey clung firmly to him, until even Job Lord was touched at the evidence of affection between the two.

While the wagon was being repaired Toby and the monkey stood hand in hand watching the work go on, while those in the cage scolded and raved because they had been induced to return to captivity. After a while the old monkey seated himself on Toby's arm and cuddled close up to him, uttering now and then a contented sort of a little squeak as the boy talked to him.

That night Mr. Stubbs slept in Toby's arms, in the band wagon, and both boy and monkey appeared very well contented with their lot, which a short time previous had seemed so hard.

When Toby awakened to his second day's work with the circus his monkey friend was seated by his side, gravely exploring his pockets, and all the boy's treasures were being spread out on the floor of the wagon by his side. Toby remonstrated with him on this breach of confidence, but Mr. Stubbs was more in the mood for sport than for grave conversation, and the more Toby talked the more mischievous did he become, until at length the boy gathered up his little store of treasures, took the monkey by the paw, and walked him toward the cage from which he had escaped on the previous night.

"Now, Mr. Stubbs," said Toby, speaking in an injured tone, "you must go in here and stay till I have got more time to fool with you."

He opened the door of the cage, but the monkey struggled as well as he was able, and Toby was obliged to exert all his strength to put him in.

When once the door was fastened upon him Toby tried to impress upon his monkey friend's mind the importance of being more

sedate, and he was convinced that the words
had sunk deep into Mr. Stubbs's heart, for,
by the time he had concluded, the old monkey
was seated in the corner of the cage, looking
up from under his shaggy eyebrows in the
most reproachful manner possible.

Toby felt sorry that he had spoken so
harshly, and was about to make amends for
his severity, when Mr. Lord's gruff voice
recalled him to the fact that his time was not
his own, and he therefore commenced his
day's work, but with a lighter heart than he
had had since he stole away from Uncle
Daniel and Guilford.

This day was not very much different from
the preceding one so far as the manner of
Mr. Lord and his partner toward the boy
was concerned; they seemed to have an idea
that he was doing only about half as much
work as he ought to, and both united in
swearing at and abusing him as much as
possible.

So far as his relations with other members
of the company were concerned, Toby now
stood in a much better position than before.
Those who had witnessed the scene told the
others how Toby had led in the monkeys on

the night previous, and nearly every member of the company had a kind word for the little fellow whose head could hardly be seen above the counter of Messrs. Lord and Jacobs's booth.

IX

THE DINNER PARTY

AT noon Toby was thoroughly tired out, for whenever anyone spoke kindly to him Mr. Lord seemed to take a malicious pleasure in giving him extra tasks to do, until Toby began to hope that no one else would pay any attention to him. On this day he was permitted to go to dinner first, and after he returned he was left in charge of the booth. Trade being dull—as it usually was during the dinner hour—he had very little work to do after he had cleaned the glasses and set things to rights generally.

When, therefore, he saw the gaunt form of the skeleton emerge from his tent and come toward him he was particularly pleased, for he had begun to think very kindly of the thin man and his fleshy wife.

"Well, Toby," said the skeleton, as he came up to the booth, carefully dusted Mr. Lord's private chair, and sat down very cautiously in it, as if he expected that it would break down under his weight, "I hear you've been making quite a hero of yourself by capturing the monkeys last night."

Toby's freckled face reddened with pleasure as he heard these words, and he stammered out, with considerable difficulty, "I didn't do anything; it was Mr. Stubbs that brought 'em back."

"Mr. Stubbs!" And the skeleton laughed so heartily that Toby was afraid he would dislocate some of his thinly covered joints. "When you was tellin' about Mr. Stubbs yesterday I thought you meant someone belonging to the company. You ought to have seen my wife Lilly shake with laughing when I told her who Mr. Stubbs was!"

"Yes," said Toby, at a loss to know just what to say, "I should think she *would* shake when she laughs."

"She does," replied the skeleton. "If you could see her when something funny strikes her you'd think she was one of those big plates of jelly that they have in the bakeshop windows." And Mr. Treat looked proudly at the gaudy picture which represented his

91

wife in all her monstrosity of flesh. "She's a great woman, Toby, an' she's got a great head."

Toby nodded his head in assent. He would have liked to say something nice regarding Mrs. Treat, but he really did not know what to say, so he simply contented himself and the fond husband by nodding.

"She thinks a good deal of you, Toby," continued the skeleton, as he moved his chair to a position more favorable for him to elevate his feet on the edge of the counter, and placed his handkerchief under him as a cushion; "she's talking of you all the time, and if you wasn't such a little fellow I should begin to be jealous of you—I should, upon my word."

"You're—both—very—good," stammered Toby, so weighted down by a sense of the honor heaped upon him as to be at a loss for words.

"An' she wants to see more of you. She made me come out here now, when she knew Mr. Lord would be away, to tell you that we're goin' to have a little kind of a friendly dinner in our tent to-morrow—she's cooked it all herself, or she's going to—and we want you to come in an' have some with us."

Toby's eyes glistened at the thought of the
unexpected pleasure, and then his face grew
sad as he replied, "I'd like to come first
rate, Mr. Treat, but I don't s'pose Mr. Lord
would let me stay away from the shop long
enough."

"Why, you won't have any work to do
to-morrow, Toby—it's Sunday."

"So it is!" said the boy, with a pleased
smile, as he thought of the day of rest which
was so near. And then he added, quickly:
"An' this is Saturday afternoon. What fun
the boys at home are havin'! You see, there
hain't any school Saturday afternoon, an'
all the fellers go out in the woods."

"And you wish you were there to go with
them, don't you?" asked the skeleton,
sympathetically.

"Indeed I do!" exclaimed Toby, quickly.
"It's twice as good as any circus that ever
was."

"But you didn't think so before you came
with us, did you?"

"I didn't know so much about circuses
then as I do now," replied the boy, sadly.

Mr. Treat saw that he was touching on a
sore subject, and one which was arousing sad

93

thoughts in his little companion's mind, and he hastened to change it at once.

"Then I can tell Lilly that you'll come, can I?"

"Oh yes, I'll be sure to be there; an' I want you to know just how good I think you both are to me."

"That's all right, Toby," said Mr. Treat, with a pleased expression on his face; "an' you may bring Mr. Stubbs with you, if you want to."

"Thank you," said Toby. "I'm sure Mr. Stubbs will be just as glad to come as I shall. But where will we be to-morrow?"

"Right here. We always stay over Sunday at the place where we show Saturday. But I must be going, or Lilly will worry her life out of her for fear I'm somewhere getting cold. She's awful careful of me, that woman is. You'll be on hand to-morrow at one o'clock, won't you?"

"Indeed I will," said Toby, emphatically, "an' I'll bring Mr. Stubbs with me, too."

With a friendly nod of his head, the skeleton hurried away to reassure his wife that he was safe and well; and before he had hardly disappeared within the tent Toby had another

caller, who was none other than his old friend
Old Ben, the driver.

"Well, my boy," shouted Ben, in his cheery,
hearty tones, "I haven't seen you since you
left the wagon so sudden last night. Did you
get shook up much?"

"Oh no," replied Toby. "You see I hain't
very big; an' then I struck in the mud; so I
got off pretty easy."

"That's a fact; an' you can thank your
lucky stars for it, too, for I've seen grown-up
men get pitched off a wagon in that way an'
break their necks doin' it. But has Job told
you where you was going to sleep to-night?
You know we stay over here till to-morrow."

"I didn't think anything about that; but I
s'pose I'll sleep in the wagon, won't I?"

"You can sleep at the hotel, if you want to;
but the beds will likely be dirty; an' if you
take my advice you'll crawl into some of the
wagons in the tent."

Ben then explained to him that, after his
work was done that night, he would not be
expected to report for duty until the time for
starting on Sunday night, and concluded his
remarks by saying:

"Now you know what your rights are, an'

7   95

don't you let Job impose on you in any way.
I'll be round here after you get through work,
an' we'll bunk in somewhere together."

The arrival of Messrs. Lord and Jacobs put
a stop to the conversation, and was the signal
for Toby's time of trial. It seemed to him,
and with good reason, that the chief delight
these men had in life was to torment him,
for neither ever spoke a pleasant word to him;
and when one was not giving him some difficult work to do, or finding fault in some way,
the other would be sure to do so; and Toby
had very little comfort from the time he
began work in the morning until he stopped
at night.

It was not until after the evening performance was over that Toby had a chance to speak
with Mr. Stubbs, and then he was so tired
that he simply took the old monkey from the
cage, nestled him under his jacket, and lay
down with him to sleep in the place which
Old Ben had selected.

When the morning came Mr. Stubbs aroused
his young master at a much earlier hour than
he would have awakened had he been left to
himself, and the two went out for a short walk
before breakfast. They went instinctively

toward the woods; and when the shade of the trees was once reached, how the two reveled in their freedom! Mr. Stubbs climbed into the trees, swung himself from one to the other by means of his tail, gathered half-ripe nuts, which he threw at his master, tried to catch the birds, and had a good time generally.

Toby, stretched at full length on the mossy bank, watched the antics of his pet, laughing boisterously at times as Mr. Stubbs would do some one thing more comical than usual, and forgot there was in this world such a thing as a circus or such a man as Job Lord. It was to Toby a morning without a flaw, and he took no heed of the time, until the sound of the church bells warned him of the lateness of the hour, reminding him at the same time of where he should be—where he would be, if he were at home with Uncle Daniel.

In the mean time the old monkey had been trying to attract his young master's attention, and, failing in his efforts, he came down from the tree, crept softly up to Toby, and nestled his head under the boy's arm.

This little act of devotion seemed to cause Toby's grief to burst forth afresh, and, clasping

97

the monkey around the neck, hugging him
close to his bosom, he sobbed:

"Oh, Mr. Stubbs, Mr. Stubbs, how lonesome we are! If we was only at Uncle Dan'l's
we'd be the two happiest people in all this
world. We could play on the hay, or go
up to the pasture, or go down to the village;
an' I'd work my fingers off if I could only be
there just once more. It was wicked for me
to run away, an' now I'm gettin' paid for it."

He hugged the monkey closely, swaying
his body to and fro, and presenting a perfect
picture of grief. The monkey, not knowing
what to make of this changed mood, cowered
whimperingly in his arms, looking up into his
face, and licking the boy's hands whenever
he had the opportunity.

It was some time before Toby's grief exhausted itself; and then, still clasping the
monkey, he hurried out of the woods toward
the town and the now thoroughly hated circus
tents.

The clocks were just striking one as Toby
entered the inclosure used by the show as a
place of performance, and, remembering his
engagement with the skeleton and his wife,
he went directly to their tent. From the odors

which assailed him as he entered, it was very
evident that a feast of no mean proportions
was in course of preparation, and Toby's keen
appetite returned in full vigor. Even the
monkey seemed affected by the odor, for he
danced about on his master's shoulder, and
chattered so that Toby was obliged to choke
him a little in order to make him present a
respectable appearance.

When Toby reached the interior of the tent
he was astonished at the extent of the preparations that were being made, and gazed around
him in surprise. The platform on which
the lean man and fat woman were in the habit
of exhibiting themselves now bore a long table,
loaded with eatables; and, from the fact that
eight or ten chairs were ranged around it,
Toby understood that he was not the only
guest invited to the feast. Some little attempt
had also been made at decoration by festoon-
ing that end of the tent where the platform
was placed with two or three flags and some
streamers, and the tent poles also were fringed
with tissue paper of the brightest colors.

Toby had only time enough to notice this
when the skeleton advanced toward him, and,
with the liveliest appearance of pleasure, said,

as he took him by the hands with a grip that made him wince:

"It gives me great joy, Mr. Tyler, to welcome you at one of our little home reunions, if one can call a tent, that is moved every day in the week, home."

Toby hardly knew whom Mr. Treat referred to when he said "Mr. Tyler"; but by the time his hands were released from the bony grasp he understood that it was himself who was spoken to.

The skeleton then formally introduced him to the other guests present, who were sitting at one end of the tent, and evidently anxiously awaiting the coming feast.

"These," said Mr. Treat, as he waved his hand toward two white-haired, pink-eyed young ladies who sat with their arms twined around each other's waist, and had been eying the monkey with some appearance of fear, "are the Miss Cushings, known to the world as the Albino Children; they command a large salary and form a very attractive feature of our exhibition."

The young ladies arose at the same time, as if they had been the Siamese Twins and could not act independently of each other, and bowed.

Toby made the best bow he was capable of; and the monkey made frantic efforts to escape, as if he would enjoy twisting his paws in their perpendicular hair.

"And this," continued Mr. Treat, pointing to a sickly, sour-looking individual who was sitting apart from the others, with his arms folded, and looking as if he was counting the very seconds before the dinner should begin, "is the wonderful Signor Castro, whose sword-swallowing feats you have doubtless heard of."

Toby stepped back just one step, as if overwhelmed by awe at beholding the signor in the guise of a humble individual; and the gentleman who gained his livelihood by swallowing swords unbent his dignity so far as to unfold his arms and present a very dirty-looking hand for Toby to shake. The boy took hold of the outstretched hand, wondering why the signor never used soap and water; and Mr. Stubbs, apparently afraid of the sour-looking man, retreated to Toby's shoulder, where he sat chattering and scolding about the introduction.

Again the skeleton waved his hand, and this time he introduced "Mademoiselle Spelletti, the wonderful snake-charmer, whose exploits in this country, and before the crowned heads of Europe had caused the whole world to stand aghast at her daring."

Mademoiselle Spelletti was a very ordinary-looking young lady of about twenty-five years of age, who looked very much as if her name might originally have been Murphy, and she, too, extended a hand for Toby to grasp—only her hand was clean, and she appeared to be a very much more pleasant acquaintance than the gentleman who swallowed swords.

This ended the introductions; and Toby was just looking around for a seat, when Mrs. Treat, the fat lady and the giver of the feast which was about to come, and which already smelled so invitingly, entered from behind a curtain of canvas, where the cooking stove was supposed to be located.

She had every appearance of being the cook for the occasion. Her sleeves were rolled up, her hair tumbled and frowzy, and there were several unmistakable marks of grease on the front of her calico dress.

She waited for no ceremony, but rushed up to Toby and, taking him in her arms, gave him such a squeeze that there seemed to be every possibility that she would break all the bones in his body; and she kept him so long in this bearlike embrace that Mr. Stubbs reached his little brown paws over and got such a hold of her hair that all present, save Signor Castro, rushed forward to release her from the monkey's grasp.

"You dear little thing!" said Mrs. Treat, paying but slight attention to the hair-pulling she had just undergone, and holding Toby at arm's length so that she could look into his face, "you were so late that I was afraid you wasn't coming; and my dinner wouldn't have tasted half so good if you hadn't been here to eat some."

Toby hardly knew what to say for this hearty welcome, and he managed to tell the large and kind-hearted lady that he had had no idea of missing the dinner, and that he was very glad she wanted him to come.

"Want you to come, you dear little thing!" she exclaimed, as she gave him another hug, but careful not to give Mr. Stubbs a chance of grasping her hair again. "Of course I wanted you to come, for this dinner has been got up so that you could meet these people here, and so that they could see you."

Toby was entirely at a loss to know what

to say to this overwhelming compliment, and
for that reason did not say anything, only
submitting patiently to the third hug, which
was all Mrs. Treat had time to give him, as
she was obliged to rush behind the canvas
screen again, as there were unmistakable
sounds of something boiling over on the stove.

"You'll excuse me," said the skeleton, with
an air of dignity, waving his hand once more
toward the assembled company, "but while
introducing you to Mr. Tyler I had almost
forgotten to introduce him to you. This,
ladies and gentlemen"—and here he touched
Toby on the shoulder, as if he were some
living curiosity whose habits and mode of
capture he was about to explain to a party of
spectators—"is Mr. Toby Tyler, of whom
you heard on the night when the monkey
cage was smashed, and who now carries with
him the identical monkey which was presented
to him by the manager of this great show as a
token of esteem for his skill and bravery in
capturing the entire lot of monkeys without
a single blow."

By the time that Mr. Treat got through
with his long speech Toby felt very much
as if he were some wonderful creature whom

the skeleton was exhibiting; but he managed to rise to his feet and duck his little red head in his best imitation of a bow. Then he sat down and hugged Mr. Stubbs to cover his confusion.

One of the Albino Children now came forward, and, while stroking Mr. Stubbs's hair, looked so intently at Toby that for the life of him he couldn't say which she regarded as the curiosity, himself or the monkey; therefore he hastened to say, modestly:

"I didn't do much toward catchin' the monkeys; Mr. Stubbs here did almost all of it, an' I only led 'em in."

"There, there, my boy," said the skeleton, in a fatherly tone, "I've heard the whole story from Old Ben, an' I sha'n't let you get out of it like that. We all know what you did, an' it's no use for you to deny any part of it."

X

MR. STUBBS AT A PARTY

TOBY was about to say that he did not intend to represent the matter other than it really was, when a voice from behind the canvas screen arrested further conversation.

"Sam-u-el, come an' help me carry these things in."

Something very like a smile of satisfaction passed over Signor Castro's face as he heard this, which told him that the time for the feast was near at hand; and the snake-charmer, as well as the Albino Children, seemed quite as much pleased as did the sword-swallower.

"You will excuse me, ladies and gentlemen," said the skeleton, in an important tone; "I must help Lilly, and then I shall have the pleasure of helping you to some of her cooking, which, if I do say it, that oughtn't, is as good as can be found in this entire country."

Then he, too, disappeared behind the canvas
screen.

Left alone, Toby looked at the ladies, and
the ladies looked at him, in perfect silence,
while the sword-swallower grimly regarded
them all, until Mr. Treat reappeared, bearing
on a platter an immense turkey, as nicely
browned as any Thanksgiving turkey Toby
ever saw. Behind him came his fat wife,
carrying several dishes, each of which emitted
a most fragrant odor; and as these were placed
upon the table the spirits of the sword-swallower seemed to revive, and he smiled pleasantly; while even the ladies appeared ani-
mated by the sight and odor of the good things
which they were to be called upon so soon to
pass judgment.

Several times did Mr. and Mrs. Treat bustle
in and out from behind the screen, and each
time they made some addition to that which
was upon the table, until Toby began to fear
that they would never finish, and the sword-
swallower seemed unable to restrain his
impatience.

At last the finishing touch had been put
to the table, the last dish placed in position,
and then, with a certain kind of grace, which

no one but a man as thin as Mr. Treat could assume, he advanced to the edge of the platform and said:

"Ladies and gentlemen, nothing gives me greater pleasure than to invite you all, including Mr. Tyler's friend Stubbs, to the bountiful repast which my Lilly has prepared for—"

At this point Mr. Treat's speech—for it certainly seemed as if he had commenced to make one—was broken off in a most summary manner. His wife had come up behind him and, with as much ease as if he had been a child, lifted him from off the floor and placed him gently in the chair at the head of the table.

"Come right up and get dinner," she said to her guests. "If you had waited until Samuel had finished his speech everything on the table would have been stone cold."

The guests proceeded to obey her kindly command; and it is to be regretted that the sword-swallower had no better manners than to jump on to the platform with one bound and seat himself at the table with the most unseemly haste. The others, and more especially Toby, proceeded in a leisurely and more dignified manner.

A seat had been placed by the side of the
one intended for Toby for the accommodation
of Mr. Stubbs, who suffered a napkin to be
tied under his chin, and behaved generally
in a manner that gladdened the heart of his
young master.

Mr. Treat cut generous slices from the
turkey for each guest, and Mrs. Treat piled
their plates high with all sorts of vegetables,
complaining, after the manner of housewives
generally, that the food was not cooked as
she would like to have had it, and declaring
that she had had poor luck with everything
that morning, when she firmly believed in her
heart that her table had never looked better.

After the company had had the edge taken
off their appetites—which effect was pro-
duced on the sword-swallower only after he
had been helped three different times, the
conversation began by the fat woman asking
Toby how he got along with Mr. Lord.

Toby could not give a very good account of
his employer, but he had the good sense not to
cast a damper on a party of pleasure by recit-
ing his own troubles; so he said, evasively:

"I guess I shall get along pretty well, now
that I have got so many friends."

Just as he had commenced to speak the skeleton had put into his mouth a very large piece of turkey—very much larger in proportion than himself—and when Toby had finished speaking he started to say something evidently not very complimentary to Mr. Lord. But what it was the company never knew; for just as he opened his mouth to speak, the food went down the wrong way, his face became a bright purple, and it was quite evident that he was choking.

Toby was alarmed, and sprang from his chair to assist his friend, upsetting Mr. Stubbs from his seat, causing him to scamper up the tent pole, with the napkin still tied around his neck, and to scold in his most vehement manner. Before Toby could reach the skeleton, however, the fat woman had darted toward her lean husband, caught him by the arm, and was pounding his back, by the time Toby got there, so vigorously that the boy was afraid her enormous hand would go through his tissue-paperlike frame.

"I wouldn't," said Toby, in alarm; "you may break him."

"Don't you get frightened," said Mrs. Treat, turning her husband completely over, and still continuing the drumming process. "He's often taken this way; he's such a glutton that he'd try to swallow the turkey whole if he could get it in his mouth, an' he's so thin that 'most anything sticks in his throat."

"I should think you'd break him all up," said Toby, apologetically, as he resumed his seat at the table; "he don't look as if he could stand very much of that sort of thing."

But apparently Mr. Treat could stand very much more than Toby gave him credit for, because at this juncture he stopped coughing, and his face fast assumed its natural hue.

His attentive wife, seeing that he had ceased struggling, lifted him in her arms and sat him down in his chair with a force that threatened to snap his head off.

"There!" she said, as he wheezed a little from the effects of the shock, "now see if you can behave yourself an' chew your meat as you ought to! One of these days when you're alone you'll try that game, and that 'll be the last of you."

"If he'd try to do one of my tricks long enough he'd get so that there wouldn't hardly anything choke him," the sword-swallower ventured to suggest, mildly, as he wiped a small stream of cranberry sauce from his chin and laid a well-polished turkey bone by the side of his plate.

"I'd like to see him try it!" said the fat lady, with just a shade of anger in her voice. Then turning toward her husband, she said, emphatically, "Samuel, don't you ever let me catch *you* swallowing a sword!"

"I won't, my love, I won't; and I will try to chew my meat more," replied the very thin glutton, in a feeble tone.

Toby thought that perhaps the skeleton might keep the first part of that promise, but he was not quite sure about the last.

It required no little coaxing on the part of both Toby and Mrs. Treat to induce Mr. Stubbs to come down from his lofty perch; but the task was accomplished at last, and by the gift of a very large doughnut he was induced to resume his seat at the table.

The time had now come when the duties of a host, in his own peculiar way of viewing them, devolved upon Mr. Treat, and he said, as he pushed his chair back a short distance from the table and tried to polish the front of his vest with his napkin:

"I don't want this fact lost sight of, because

it is an important one: everyone must remember that we have gathered here to meet and become better acquainted with the latest and best addition to this circus, Mr. Toby Tyler."

Poor Toby! As the company all looked directly at him, and Mrs. Treat nodded her enormous head energetically, as if to say that she agreed exactly with her husband, the poor boy's face grew very red and the squash pie lost its flavor.

"Although Mr. Tyler may not be exactly one of us, owing to the fact that he does not belong to the profession, but is only one of the adjuncts to it, so to speak," continued the skeleton, in a voice which was fast being raised to its highest pitch, "we feel proud, after his exploits at the time of the accident, to have him with us, and gladly welcome him now, through the medium of this little feast prepared by my Lilly."

Here the Albino Children nodded their heads in approval, and the sword-swallower gave a grunt of assent; and, thus encouraged, the skeleton proceeded:

"I feel, when I say that we like and admire Mr. Tyler, all present will agree with me and all would like to hear him say a word for himself."

The skeleton seemed to have expressed the views of those present remarkably well, judging from their expressions of pleasure and assent, and all waited for the honored guest to speak.

Toby knew that he must say something, but he couldn't think of a single thing; he tried over and over again to call to his mind something which he had read as to how people acted and what they said when they were expected to speak at a dinner table, but his thoughts refused to go back for him, and the silence was actually becoming painful. Finally, and with the greatest effort, he managed to say, with a very perceptible stammer, and while his face was growing very red:

"I know I ought to say something to pay for this big dinner that you said was gotten up for me, but I don't know what to say, unless to thank you for it. You see, I hain't big enough to say much, an', as Uncle Dan'l says, I don't amount to very much, 'cept for eatin', an' I guess he's right. You're all real good to me, an' when I get to be a man I'll try to do as much for you."

Toby had risen to his feet when he began
to make his speech, and while he was speaking
Mr. Stubbs had crawled over into his chair.
When he finished he sat down again without
looking behind him, and of course sat plump
on the monkey. There was a loud outcry
from Mr. Stubbs, a little frightened noise
from Toby, an instant's scrambling, and then
boy, monkey, and chair tumbled off the platform, landing on the ground in an indescrib-
able mass, from which the monkey extricated
himself more quickly than Toby could, and
again took refuge on the top of the tent pole.

Of course all the guests ran to Toby's
assistance; and while the fat woman poked
him all over to see that none of his bones
were broken, the skeleton brushed the dirt
from his clothes.

All this time the monkey screamed, yelled,
and danced around on the tent pole and ropes,
as if his feelings had received a shock from
which he could never recover.

"I didn't mean to end it up that way, but
it was Mr. Stubbs's fault," said Toby, as soon
as quiet had been restored and the guests,
with the exception of the monkey, were seated
at the table once more.

"Of course you didn't," said Mrs. Treat, in a kindly tone. "But don't you feel bad about it one bit, for you ought to thank your lucky stars that you didn't break any of your bones."

"I s'pose I had," said Toby, soberly, as he looked back at the scene of his disaster, and then up at the chattering monkey that had caused all the trouble.

Shortly after this, Mr. Stubbs having again been coaxed down from his lofty position, Toby took his departure, promising to call as often during the week as he could get away from his exacting employers.

Just outside the tent he met Old Ben, who said, as he showed signs of indulging in another of his internal laughing spells:

"Hello! has the skeleton an' his lily of a wife been givin' a blow-out to you, too?"

"They invited me in there to dinner," said Toby, modestly.

"Of course they did—of course they did," replied Ben, with a chuckle; "they carries a cookin' stove along with 'em, so's they can give these little spreads whenever we stay over a day in a place. Oh, I've been there!"

"And did they ask you to make a speech?"

"Of course. Did they try it on you?"

"Yes," said Toby, mournfully, "an' I tumbled off the platform when I got through."

"I didn't do exactly that," replied Ben, thoughtfully; "but I s'pose you got too much steam on, seein' 's how it was likely your first speech. Now you'd better go into the tent an' try to get a little sleep, 'cause we've got a long ride to-night over a rough road, an' you won't get more 'n a cat nap all night."

"But where are you going?" asked Toby, as he shifted Mr. Stubbs over to his other shoulder, preparatory to following his friend's advice.

"I'm goin' to church," said Ben, and then Toby noticed for the first time that the old driver had made some attempt at dressing up. "I've been with the circus, man an' boy, for nigh to forty years, an' I allus go to meetin' once on Sunday. It's somethin' I promised my old mother I would do, an' I hain't broke my promise yet."

"Why don't you take me with you?" asked Toby, wistfully, as he thought of the little church on the hill at home, and wished—oh, so earnestly!—that he was there then, even at the risk of being thumped on the head with Uncle Daniel's book.

"If I'd seen you this mornin' I would," said Ben; "but now you must try to bottle up some sleep ag'in' to-night, an' next Sunday I'll take you."

With these words Old Ben started off, and Toby proceeded to carry out his wishes, although he rather doubted the possibility of "bottling up" any sleep that afternoon.

He lay down on the top of the wagon, after having put Mr. Stubbs inside, with the others of his tribe, and in a very few moments the boy was sound asleep, dreaming of a dinner party at which Mr. Stubbs made a speech and he himself scampered up and down the tent pole.

XI

A STORMY NIGHT

WHEN Toby awoke it was nearly dark, and the bustle around him told very plainly that the time for departure was near at hand. He rubbed his eyes just enough to make sure that he was thoroughly awake, and then jumped down from his rather lofty bed, and ran around to the door of the cage to assure himself that Mr. Stubbs was safe. This done, his preparations for the journey were made.

Now Toby noticed that each one of the drivers was clad in rubber clothing, and, after listening for a moment, he learned the cause of their waterproof garments. It was raining very hard, and Toby thought with dismay of the long ride that he would have to take on the top of the monkeys' cage, with no protection whatever save that afforded by his ordinary clothing.

While he was standing by the side of his wagon, wondering how he should get along, Old Ben came in. The water was pouring from his clothes in little rivulets, and he afforded most unmistakable evidence of the damp state of the weather.

"It's a nasty night, my boy," said the old driver, in much the same cheery tone that he would have used had he been informing Toby that it was a beautiful moonlight evening.

"I guess I'll get wet," said Toby, ruefully, as he looked up at the lofty seat which he was to occupy.

"Bless me!" said Ben, as if the thought had just come to him, "it won't do for you to ride outside on a night like this. You wait here, an' I'll see what I can do for you."

The old man hurried off to the other end of the tent, and almost before Toby thought he had time to go as far as the ring he returned.

"It's all right," he said, and this time in a gruff voice, as if he were announcing some misfortune; "you're to ride in the women's wagon. Come with me."

Toby followed without a question, though he was wholly at a loss to understand what the "women's wagon" was, for he had never seen anything which looked like one.

He soon learned, however, when Old Ben stopped in front—or, rather, at the end—of a long, covered wagon that looked like an omnibus, except that it was considerably longer, and the seats inside were divided by arms, padded, to make them comfortable to lean against.

"Here's the boy," said Ben, as he lifted Toby up on the step, gave him a gentle push to intimate that he was to get inside, and then left him.

As Toby stepped inside he saw that the wagon was nearly full of women and children; and fearing lest he should take a seat that belonged to someone else, he stood in the middle of the wagon, not knowing what to do.

"Why don't you sit down, little boy?" asked one of the ladies, after Toby had remained standing nearly five minutes and the wagon was about to start.

"Well," said Toby, with some hesitation, as he looked around at the two or three empty seats that remained, "I didn't want to get in anybody else's place an' I didn't know where to sit."

"Come right here," said the lady, as she pointed to a seat by the side of a little girl who did not look any older than Toby; "the lady who usually occupies that seat will not be here to-night, and you can have it."

"Thank you, ma'am," said Toby, as he sat timidly down on the edge of the seat, hardly daring to sit back comfortably, and feeling very awkward meanwhile, but congratulating himself on being thus protected from the pouring rain.

The wagon started, and as each one talked with her neighbor, Toby felt a most dismal sense of loneliness, and almost wished that he was riding on the monkey cart with Ben, where he could have someone to talk with. He gradually pushed himself back into a more comfortable position, and had then an opportunity of seeing more plainly the young girl who rode by his side.

She was quite as young as Toby, and small of her age; but there was an old look about her face that made the boy think of her as being an old woman cut down to fit children's clothes. Toby had looked at her so earnestly that she observed him, and asked, "What is your name?"

"Toby Tyler."

"What do you do in the circus?"

"Sell candy for Mr. Lord."

"Oh! I thought you was a new member of the company."

Toby knew by the tone of her voice that he had fallen considerably in her estimation by not being one of the performers, and it was some little time before he ventured to speak; and then he asked, timidly. "What do you do?"

"I ride one of the horses with mother."

"Are you the little girl that comes out with the lady an' four horses?" asked Toby, in awe that he should be conversing with so famous a person.

"Yes, I am. Don't I do it nicely?"

"Why, you're a perfect little—little—fairy!" exclaimed Toby, after hesitating a moment to find some word which would exactly express his idea.

This praise seemed to please the young lady, and in a short time the two became very good friends, even if Toby did not occupy a more exalted position than that of candy seller. She had learned from him all about the accident to the monkey cage, and about Mr.

Stubbs, and in return had told him that her name was Ella Mason, though on the bills she was called "Mademoiselle Jeannette."

For a long time the two children sat talking together, and then Mademoiselle Jeannette curled herself up on the seat, with her head in her mother's lap, and went to sleep.

Toby had resolved to keep awake and watch her, for he was struck with admiration at her face; but sleep got the better of him in less than five minutes after he had made the resolution, and he sat bolt upright, with his little round head nodding and bobbing until it seemed almost certain that he would shake it off.

When Toby awoke the wagon was drawn up by the side of the road, the sun was shining brightly, preparations were being made for the entrée into town, and the harsh voice of Mr. Job Lord was shouting his name in a tone that boded no good for poor Toby when he should make his appearance.

Toby would have hesitated before meeting his angry employer but that he knew it would only make matters worse for him when he did show himself, and he mentally braced himself for the trouble which he knew was coming. The little girl whose acquaintance he had made the night previous was still sleeping; and, wishing to say good-by to her in some way without awakening her, he stooped down and gently kissed the skirt of her dress. Then he went out to meet his master.

Mr. Lord was thoroughly enraged when Toby left the wagon, and saw the boy just as he stepped to the ground. The angry man gave a quick glance around, to make sure that none of Toby's friends were in sight, and then caught him by the coat collar and commenced to whip him severely with the small rubber cane that he usually carried.

Mr. Job Lord lifted the poor boy entirely clear of the ground, and each blow that he struck could be heard almost the entire length of the circus train.

"You've been makin' so many acquaintances here that you hain't willin' to do any work," he said, savagely, as he redoubled the force of his blows.

"Oh, please stop! please stop!" shrieked the poor boy in his agony. "I'll do everything you tell me to, if you won't strike me again!"

This piteous appeal seemed to have no

effect upon the cruel man, and he continued to whip the boy, despite his cries
and entreaties, until his arm fairly ached
from the exertion and Toby's body was
crossed and recrossed with the livid marks
of the cane.

"Now let's see whether you'll 'tend to
your work or not!" said the man as he flung
Toby from him with such force that the boy
staggered, reeled, and nearly fell into the
little brook that flowed by the roadside.
"I'll make you understand that all the
friends you've whined around in this show
can't save you from a lickin' when I get
ready to give you one! Now go an' do
your work that ought to have been done
an hour ago!"

Mr. Lord walked away with the proud con-
sciousness of a man who has achieved a great
victory, and Toby was limping painfully
along toward the cart that was used in con-
veying Mr. Lord's stock in trade, when he
felt a tiny hand slip into his and heard a
childish voice say:

"Don't cry, Toby. Sometime, when I get
big enough, I'll make Mr. Lord sorry that he
whipped you as he did; and I'm big enough

now to tell him just what kind of a man I think he is."

Looking around, Toby saw his little acquaintance of the evening previous, and he tried to force back the big tears that were rolling down his cheeks as he said, in a voice choked with grief: "You're awful good, an' I don't mind the lickin' when you say you're sorry for me. I s'pose I deserve it for runnin' away from Uncle Dan'l."

"Did it hurt you much?" she asked, feelingly.

"It did when he was doin' it," replied Toby, manfully, "but it don't a bit, now that you've come."

"Then I'll go and talk to that Mr. Lord, and I'll come and see you again after we get into town," said the little miss, as she hurried away to tell the candy vender what she thought of him.

That day, as on all others since he had been with the circus, Toby went to his work with a heavy heart, and time and time again did he count the money which had been given him by kind-hearted strangers, to see whether he had enough to warrant his attempting to run away. Three dollars and twenty-five cents was the total amount of his treasure, and, large as that sum appeared to him, he could not satisfy himself that he had sufficient to enable him to get back to the home which he had so wickedly left. Whenever he thought of this home, of the Uncle Daniel who had in charity cared for him—a motherless, father-less boy—and of returning to it, with not even as much right as the Prodigal Son, of whom he had heard Uncle Daniel tell, his heart sank within him and he doubted whether he would be allowed to remain even if he should be so fortunate as ever to reach Guilford again.

This day passed, so far as Toby was con-cerned, very much as had the others: he could not satisfy either of his employers, try as hard as he might; but, as usual, he met with two or three kindly disposed people, who added to the fund that he was accumu-lating for his second venture of running away by little gifts of money, each one of which gladdened his heart and made his trouble a trifle less hard to bear.

During the entire week he was thus equally fortunate. Each day added something to his fund, and each night it seemed to Toby that he was one day nearer the freedom for which he so ardently longed.

The skeleton, the fat lady, Old Ben, the Albino Children, little Ella, and even the sword-swallower, all gave him a kindly word as they passed him while he was at his work, or saw him as the preparations for the grand entrée were being made.

The time had passed slowly to Toby, and yet Sunday came again—as Sundays always come; and on this day Old Ben hunted him up, made him wash his face and hands until they fairly shone from very cleanliness, and then took him to church. Toby was surprised to find that it was really a pleasant thing to be able to go to church after being deprived of it, and was more light-hearted than he had yet been since he left Guilford when he returned to the tent at noon.

The skeleton had invited him to another dinner party, but Toby had declined the invitation, agreeing to present himself in time for supper instead. He hardly cared to go through the ordeal of another state dinner; and besides, he wanted to go off to the woods with the old monkey, where he could enjoy the silence of the forest, which seemed like a friend to him, because it reminded him of home.

Taking the monkey with him as usual, he inquired the nearest way to a grove, and, without waiting for dinner, started off for an afternoon's quiet enjoyment.

XII

TOBY'S GREAT MISFORTUNE

THE town in which the circus remained over Sunday was a small one, and a brisk walk of ten minutes sufficed to take Toby into a secluded portion of a very thickly grown wood, where he could lie upon the mossy ground and fairly revel in freedom.

As he lay upon his back, his hands under his head, and his eyes directed to the branches of the trees above, where the birds twittered and sung, and the squirrels played in fearless sport, the monkey enjoyed himself, in his way, by playing all the monkey antics he knew of. He scrambled from tree to tree, swung himself from one branch to the other by the aid of his tail, and amused both himself and his master, until, tired by his exertions, he crept down by Toby's side and lay there in quiet, restful content.

One of Toby's reasons for wishing to be by

himself that afternoon was that he wanted to think over some plan of escape, for he believed that he had nearly money enough to enable him to make a bold stroke for freedom and Uncle Daniel's. Therefore, when the monkey nestled down by his side he was all ready to confide in him that which had been occupying his busy little brain for the past three days.

"Mr. Stubbs," he said to the monkey, in a solemn tone, "we're goin' to run away in a day or two."

Mr. Stubbs did not seem to be moved in the least at this very startling piece of intelligence, but winked his bright eyes in unconcern; and Toby, seeming to think that everything which he said had been understood by the monkey, continued: "I've got a good deal of money now, an' I guess there's enough for us to start out on. We'll get away some night, an' stay in the woods till they get through hunting for us, an' then we'll go back to Guilford an' tell Uncle Dan'l if he'll only take us back we'll never go to sleep in meetin' any more, an' we'll be just as good as we know how. Now let's see how much money we've got."

Toby drew from a pocket, which he had

been at a great deal of trouble to make in his shirt, a small bag of silver, and spread it upon the ground, where he could count it at his leisure.

The glittering coin instantly attracted the monkey's attention, and he tried by every means to thrust his little black paw into the pile; but Toby would allow nothing of that sort, and pushed him away quite roughly. Then he grew excited, and danced and scolded around Toby's treasure until the boy had hard work to count it.

He did succeed, however, and as he carefully replaced it in the bag he said to the monkey: "There's seven dollars an' thirty cents in that bag, an' every cent of it is mine. That ought to take care of us for a good while, Mr. Stubbs; an' by the time we get home we shall be rich men."

The monkey showed his pleasure at this intelligence by putting his hand inside Toby's clothes to find the bag of treasure that he had seen secreted there, and two or three times, to the great delight of both himself and the boy, he drew forth the bag, which was immediately taken away from him.

The shadows were beginning to lengthen

in the woods, and, heeding this warning of the coming night, Toby took the monkey on his arm and started for home, or for the tent, which was the only place he could call home.

As he walked along he tried to talk to his pet in a serious manner, but the monkey, remembering where he had seen the bright coins secreted, tried so hard to get at them that finally Toby lost all patience and gave him quite a hard cuff on the ear, which had the effect of keeping him quiet for a time.

That night Toby took supper with the skeleton and his wife, and he enjoyed the meal, even though it was made from what had been left of the turkey that served as the noonday feast, more than he did the state dinner, where he was obliged to pay for what he ate by the torture of making a speech.

There were no guests but Toby present; and Mr. and Mrs. Treat were not only very kind, but so attentive that he was actually afraid he should eat so much as to stand in need of some of the catnip tea which Mrs. Treat had said she gave to her husband when he had been equally foolish. The skeleton would pile his plate high with turkey bones from one side, and the fat lady would heap it

134

up, whenever she could find a chance, with all sorts of food from the other, until Toby pushed back his chair, his appetite completely satisfied, if it never had been so before.

Toby had discussed the temper of his employer with his host and hostess, and, after some considerable conversation, confided in them his determination to run away.

"I'd hate awfully to have you go," said Mrs. Treat, reflectively; "but it's a good deal better for you to get away from that Job Lord if you can. It wouldn't do to let him know that you had any idea of goin', for he'd watch you as a cat watches a mouse, an' never let you go so long as he saw a chance to keep you. I heard him tellin' one of the drivers the other day that you sold more goods than any other boy he ever had, an' he was going to keep you with him all summer."

"Be careful in what you do, my boy," said the skeleton, sagely, as he arranged a large cushion in an armchair, and proceeded to make ready for his after-dinner nap; "be sure that you're all ready before you start, an', when you do go, get a good ways ahead of him; for if he should ever catch you the trouncin' you'd get would be awful."

135

Toby assured his friends that he would use every endeavor to make his escape successful when he did start; and Mrs. Treat, with an eye to the boy's comfort, said, "Let me know the night you're goin', an' I'll fix you up something to eat, so's you won't be hungry before you come to a place where you can buy something."

As these kind-hearted people talked with him, and were ready thus to aid him in every way that lay in their power, Toby thought that he had been very fortunate in thus having made so many kind friends in a place where he was having so much trouble.

It was not until he heard the sounds of preparation for departure that he left the skeleton's tent, and then, with Mr. Stubbs clasped tightly to his breast, he hurried over to the wagon where Old Ben was nearly ready to start.

"All right, Toby," said the old driver, as the boy came in sight. "I was afraid you was goin' to keep me waitin' for the first time. Jump right up on the box, for there hain't no time to lose, an' I guess you'll have to carry the monkey in your arms, for I don't want to stop to open the cage now."

"I'd just as soon carry him, an' a little rather," said Toby, as he clambered up on the high seat and arranged a comfortable place in his lap for his pet to sit.

In another moment the heavy team had started, and nearly the entire circus was on the move. "Now tell me what you've been doin' since I left you," said Old Ben, after they were well clear of the town and he could trust his horses to follow the team ahead. "I s'pose you've been to see the skeleton an' his mountain of a wife?"

Toby gave a clear account of where he had been and what he had done, and when he concluded he told Old Ben of his determination to run away, and asked his advice on the matter.

"My advice," said Ben, after he had waited some time, to give due weight to his words, "is that you clear out from this show just as soon as you can. This hain't no fit place for a boy of your age to be in, an' the sooner you get back where you started from, an' get to school, the better. But Job Lord will do all he can to keep you from goin', if he thinks you have any idea of leavin' him."

Toby assured Ben, as he had assured the

skeleton and his wife, that he would be very careful in all he did, and lay his plans with the utmost secrecy; and then he asked whether Ben thought the amount of money which he had would be sufficient to carry him home.

"Waal, that depends," said the driver, slowly. "If you go to spreadin' yourself all over creation, as boys are very apt to do, your money won't go very far; but if you look at your money two or three times afore you spend it, you ought to get back and have a dollar or two left."

The two talked, and Old Ben offered advice, until Toby could hardly keep his eyes open, and almost before the driver concluded his sage remarks the boy had stretched himself on the top of the wagon, where he had learned to sleep without being shaken off, and was soon in dreamland.

The monkey, nestled down snug in Toby's bosom, did not appear to be as sleepy as was his master, but popped his head in and out from under the coat, as if watching whether the boy was asleep or not.

Toby was awakened by a scratching on his face, as if the monkey was dancing a hornpipe on that portion of his body, and by a shrill, quick chattering, which caused him to assume an upright position instantly.

He was frightened, although he knew not at what, and looked around quickly to discover the cause of the monkey's excitement.

Old Ben was asleep on his box, while the horses jogged along behind the other teams, and Toby failed to see anything whatever which should have caused his pet to become so excited.

"Lie down an' behave yourself," said Toby, as sternly as possible, and as he spoke he took his pet by the collar, to oblige him to obey his command.

The moment that he did this he saw the monkey throw something out into the road, and the next instant he also saw that he held something tightly clutched in his other paw.

It required some little exertion and active movement on Toby's part to enable him to get hold of that paw, in order to discover what it was which Mr. Stubbs had captured; but the instant he did succeed, there went up from his heart such a cry of sorrow as caused Old Ben to start up in alarm and the monkey to cower and whimper like a whipped dog.

139

"What is it, Toby? What's the matter?" asked the old driver, as he peered out into the darkness ahead, as if he feared some danger threatened them from that quarter. "I don't see anything. What is it?"

"Mr. Stubbs has thrown all my money away," cried Toby, holding up the almost empty bag, which a short time previous had been so well filled with silver.

"Stubbs—thrown—the—money—away?" repeated Ben, with a pause between each word, as if he could not understand that which he himself was saying.

"Yes," sobbed Toby, as he shook out the remaining contents of the bag, "there's only half a dollar, an' all the rest is gone."

"The rest gone!" again repeated Ben. "But how come the monkey to have the money?"

"He tried to get at it out in the woods, an' I s'pose the moment I got asleep he felt for it in my pockets. This is all there is left, an' he threw away some just as I woke up."

Again Toby held the bag up where Ben could see it, and again his grief broke out anew.

Ben could say nothing; he realized the whole situation—that the monkey had got the money-bag while Toby was sleeping; that in his play he had thrown it away piece by piece; and he knew that that small amount of silver represented liberty in the boy's eyes. He felt that there was nothing he could say which would assuage Toby's grief, and he remained silent.

"Don't you s'pose we could go back an' get it?" asked the boy, after the intensity of his grief had somewhat subsided.

"No, Toby, it's gone," replied Ben, sorrowfully. "You couldn't find it if it was daylight, an' you don't stand a ghost of a chance now in the dark. Don't take on so, my boy. I'll see if we can't make it up to you in some way."

Toby gave no heed to this last remark of Ben's. He hugged the monkey convulsively to his breast, as if he would seek consolation from the very one who had wrought the ruin, and, rocking himself to and fro, he said, in a voice full of tears and sorrow:

"Oh, Mr. Stubbs, why did you do it?—why did you do it? That money would have got us away from this hateful place, an' we'd have gone back to Uncle Dan'l's, where we'd have been *so* happy, you an' me. An' now it's all

gone—all gone. What made you, Mr. Stubbs—
what made you do such a bad, cruel thing?
Oh, what made you?"

"Don't, Toby—don't take on so," said Ben,
soothingly. "There wasn't so very much
money there, after all, an' you'll soon get as
much more."

"But it won't be for a good while, an' we
could have been in the good old home long
before I can get so much again."

"That's true, my boy; but you must kinder
brace up an' not give way so about it. Perhaps I can fix it so the fellers will make it up
to you. Give Stubbs a good poundin', an'
perhaps that 'll make you feel better."

"That won't bring back my money an' I
don't want to whip him," cried Toby, hugging
his pet the closer because of this suggestion.
"I know what it is to get a whippin', an' I
wouldn't whip a dog, much less Mr. Stubbs,
who didn't know any better."

"Then you must try to take it like a man,"
said Ben, who could think of no other plan by
which the boy might soothe his feelings.
"It hain't half so bad as it might be, an' you
must try to keep a stiff upper lip, even if it
does seem hard at first."

This keeping a stiff upper lip in the face of all the trouble he was having was all very well to talk about, but Toby could not reduce it to practice, or, at least, not so soon after he knew of his loss, and he continued to rock the monkey back and forth, to whisper in his ear now and then, and to cry as if his heart was breaking, for nearly an hour.

Ben tried, in his rough, honest way, to comfort him, but without success; and it was not until the boy's grief had spent itself that he would listen to any reasoning.

All this time the monkey had remained perfectly quiet, submitting to Toby's squeezing without making any effort to get away, and behaving as if he knew he had done wrong, and was trying to atone for it. He looked up into the boy's face every now and then with such a penitent expression that Toby finally assured him of forgiveness and begged him not to feel so badly.

XIII

TOBY ATTEMPTS TO RESIGN HIS SITUATION

AT last it was possible for Toby to speak of his loss with some degree of calmness, and then he immediately began to reckon up what he could have done with the money if he had not lost it.

"Now see here, Toby," said Ben, earnestly, "don't go to doin' anything of that kind. The money's lost, an' you can't get it back by talkin'; so the very best thing for you is to stop thinkin' what you could do if you had it, an' just to look at it as a goner."

"But—" persisted Toby.

"I tell you there's no buts about it," said Ben, rather sharply. "Stop talkin' about what's gone, an' just go to thinkin' how you'll get more. Do what you've a mind to the monkey, but don't keep broodin' over what you can't help."

Toby knew that the advice was good and

he struggled manfully to carry it into execution, but it was very hard work. At all events, there was no sleep for his eyes that night; and when, just about daylight, the train halted to wait a more seasonable hour in which to enter the town, the thought of what he might have done with his lost money was still in Toby's mind.

Only once did he speak crossly to the monkey, and that was when he put him into the cage preparatory to commencing his morning's work. Then he said:

"You wouldn't had to go into this place many times more if you hadn't been so wicked, for by to-morrow night we'd been away from this circus an' on the way to home an' Uncle Dan'l. Now you've spoiled my chance an' your own for a good while to come, an' I hope before the day is over you'll feel as bad about it as I do."

It seemed to Toby as if the monkey understood just what he said to him, for he sneaked over into one corner, away from the other monkeys, and sat there looking very penitent and very dejected.

Then, with a heavy heart, Toby began his day's work.

Hard as had been Toby's lot previous to losing his money, and difficult as it had been to bear the cruelty of Mr. Job Lord and his precious partner, Mr. Jacobs, it was doubly hard now while this sorrow was fresh upon him.

Previous to this, when he had been kicked or cursed by one or the other of the partners, Toby thought exultantly that the time was not very far distant when he should be beyond the reach of his brutal taskmasters, and that thought had given him strength to bear all that had been put upon him.

Now the time of his deliverance from this bondage seemed very far off, and each cruel word or blow caused him the greater sorrow, because of the thought that but for the monkey's wickedness he would have been nearly free from that which made his life so very miserable.

If he had looked sad and mournful before, he looked doubly so now, as he went his dreary round of the tent, crying, "Here's your cold lemonade," or "Fresh-baked peanuts, ten cents a quart"; and each day there were some in the audience who pitied the boy because of the misery which showed so plainly in his

face, and they gave him a few cents more
than his price for what he was selling, or gave
him money without buying anything at all,
thereby aiding him to lay up something again
toward making his escape.

Those few belonging to the circus who knew
of Toby's intention to escape tried their best
to console him for the loss of his money, and
that kind-hearted couple, the skeleton and
his fat wife, tried to force him to take a portion of their scanty earnings in the place of
that which the monkey had thrown away.
But this Toby positively refused to do; and
to the arguments which they advanced as
reasons why they should help him along he
only replied that until he could get the money
by his own exertions he would remain with
Messrs. Lord and Jacobs and get along as
best he could.

Every hour in the day the thought of what
might have been if he had not lost his money
so haunted his mind that finally he resolved
to make one bold stroke and tell Mr. Job
Lord that he did not want to travel with the
circus any longer.

As yet he had not received the two dollars
which had been promised him for his two

weeks' work, and another one was nearly due. If he could get this money it might, with what he had saved again, suffice to pay his railroad fare to Guilford; and if it would not, he resolved to accept from the skeleton sufficient to make up the amount needed.

He naturally shrank from the task; but the hope that he might possibly succeed gave him the necessary amount of courage, and when he had gotten his work done, on the third morning after he had lost his money, and Mr. Lord appeared to be in an unusually good temper, he resolved to try the plan.

It was just before the dinner hour. Trade had been exceptionally good, and Mr. Lord had even spoken in a pleasant tone to Toby when he told him to fill up the lemonade pail with water, so that the stock might not be disposed of too quickly and with too little profit.

Toby poured in quite as much water as he thought the already weak mixture could receive and retain any flavor of lemon; and then, as his employer motioned him to add more, he mixed another quart in, secretly wondering what it would taste like.

"When you're mixin' lemonade for circus

trade," said Mr. Lord, in such a benign, fatherly tone that one would have found it difficult to believe that he ever spoke harshly, "don't be afraid of water, for there's where the profit comes in. Always have a piece of lemon peel floatin' on the top of every glass, an' it tastes just as good to people as if it cost twice as much."

Toby could not agree exactly with that opinion, neither did he think it wise to disagree, more especially since he was going to ask the very great favor of being discharged; therefore he nodded his head gravely, and began to stir up what it pleased Mr. Lord to call lemonade, so that the last addition might be more thoroughly mixed with the others.

Two or three times he attempted to ask the favor which seemed such a great one, and each time the words stuck in his throat, until it seemed to him that he should never succeed in getting them out.

Finally, in his despair, he stammered out:

"Don't you think you could find another boy in this town, Mr. Lord?"

Mr. Lord moved round sideways, in order to bring his crooked eye to bear squarely on 'Toby, and then there was a long interval of silence, during which time the boy's color rapidly came and went and his heart beat very fast with suspense and fear.

"Well, what if I could?" he said, at length. "Do you think that trade is so good I could afford to keep two boys, when there isn't half work enough for one?"

Toby stirred the lemonade with renewed activity, as if by this process he was making both it and his courage stronger, and said, in a low voice, which Mr. Lord could scarcely hear:

"I didn't think that; but you see I ought to go home, for Uncle Dan'l will worry about me; an', besides, I don't like a circus very well."

Again there was silence on Mr. Lord's part, and again the crooked eye glowered down on Toby.

"So," he said—and Toby could see that his anger was rising very fast—"you don't like a circus very well, an' you begin to think that your uncle Daniel will worry about you, eh? Well, I want you to understand that it don't make any difference to me whether you like a circus or not, and I don't care how much your uncle Daniel worries. You mean that you

want to get away from me, after I've been to
all the trouble and expense of teaching you
the business?"

Toby bent his head over the pail and stirred
away as if for dear life.

"If you think you're going to get away
from here until you've paid me for all you've
eat, an' all the time I've spent on you, you're
mistaken, that's all. You've had an easy
time with me—too easy, in fact—and that's
what ails you. Now you just let me hear
two words more out of your head about going
away—only two more—an' I'll show you what
a whipping is. I've only been playing with
you before when you thought you were getting
a whipping; but you'll find out what it means
if I so much as see a thought in your eyes
about goin' away. An' don't you dare to
try to give me the slip in the night an' run
away; for if you do I'll follow you an' have
you arrested. Now you mind your eye in
the future."

It is impossible to say how much longer
Mr. Lord might have continued this tirade
had not a member of the company—one of
the principal riders—called him one side to
speak with him.

Poor Toby was so much confused by the angry words which had followed his very natural and certainly very reasonable suggestion that he paid no attention to anything around him until he heard his own name mentioned; and then, fearing lest some new misfortune was about to befall him, he listened intently.

"I'm afraid you couldn't do much of anything with him," he heard Mr. Lord say. "He's had enough of this kind of life already, so he says, an' I expect the next thing he does will be to try and run away."

"I'll risk his getting away from you, Job," he heard the other say; "but of course I've got to take my chances. I'll take him in hand from eleven to twelve each day—just your slack time of trade—and I'll not only give you half of what he can earn in the next two years, but I'll pay you for his time, if he gives you the slip before the season is out."

Toby knew that they were speaking of him, but what it all meant he could not imagine.

"What are you going to do with him first?" Job asked.

"Just put him right in the ring and teach him what riding is. I tell you, Job, the boy's

smart enough, and before the season's over
I'll have him so that he can do some of the
bareback acts, and perhaps we'll get some
money out of him before we go into winter
quarters."

Toby understood the meaning of their conversation only too well, and he knew that his
lot, which before seemed harder than he could
bear, was about to be intensified through this
Mr. Castle, of whom he had frequently heard,
and who was said to be a rival of Mr. Lord's
so far as brutality went. The two men now
walked toward the large tent, and Toby was
left alone with his thoughts and two or three
little boy customers, who looked at him wonderingly and envied him because he belonged
to the circus.

During the ride that night he told Old Ben
what he had heard, confidently expecting
that that friend at least would console him;
but Ben was not the champion which he had
expected. The old man, who had been with a
circus, "man and boy, nigh to forty years,"
did not seem to think it any calamity that he
was to be taught to ride.

"That Mr. Castle is a little rough on boys,"
Old Ben said, thoughtfully; "but it 'll be a

good thing for you, Toby. Just so long as you stay with Job you won't be nothin' more 'n a candy-boy; but after you know how to ride it 'll be another thing, an' you can earn a good deal of money an' be your own boss."

"But I don't want to stay with the circus," whined Toby; "I don't want to learn to ride, an' I do want to get back to Uncle Dan'l."

"That may all be true, an' I don't dispute it," said Ben; "but you see you didn't stay with your uncle Daniel when you had the chance, an' you did come with the circus. You've told Job you wanted to leave, an' he 'll be watchin' you all the time to see that you don't give him the slip. Now what's the consequence? Why, you can't get away for a while, anyhow, an' you'd better try to amount to something while you are here. Perhaps after you've got so you can ride you may want to stay; an' I'll see to it that you get all of your wages, except enough to pay Castle for learnin' of you."

"I sha'n't want to stay," said Toby. "I wouldn't stay if I could ride all the horses at once an' was gettin' a hundred dollars a day."

"But you can t ride one horse, an' you
hain't gettin' but a dollar a week, an' still
I don't see any chance of your gettin' away
yet awhile," said Ben, in a matter-of-fact
tone, as he devoted his attention again to his
horses, leaving Toby to his own sad reflections
and the positive conviction that boys who
run away from home do not have a good time,
except in stories.

The next forenoon, while Toby was deep
in the excitement of selling to a boy no larger
than himself, and with just as red hair, three
cents' worth of peanuts and two sticks of
candy, and while the boy was trying to induce
him to "throw in" a piece of gum, because
of the quantity purchased, Job Lord called
him aside, and Toby knew that his troubles
had begun.

"I want you to go in an' see Mr. Castle;
he's goin' to show you how to ride," said Mr.
Lord, in as kindly a tone as if he were con-
ferring some favor on the boy.

If Toby had dared to, he would have re-
belled then and there and refused to go; but,
as he hadn't the courage for such proceeding,
he walked meekly into the tent and toward
the ring.

12   155

XIV

MR. CASTLE TEACHES TOBY TO RIDE

WHEN Toby got within sight of the ring
he was astonished at what he saw. A
horse, with a broad wooden saddle, was being
led slowly around the ring; Mr. Castle was
standing on one side, with a long whip in his
hand; and on the tent pole, which stood in
the center of the ring, was a long arm, from
which dangled a leathern belt attached to a
long rope that was carried through the end of
the arm and run down to the base of the pole.

Toby knew well enough why the horse,
the whip, and the man were there, but the
wooden projection from the tent pole, which
looked so much like a gallows, he could not
understand at all.

"Come, now," said Mr. Castle, cracking
his whip ominously as Toby came in sight,
"why weren't you here before?"

"Mr. Lord just sent me in," said Toby, not

expecting that his excuse would be received, for they never had been since he had arrived at the height of his ambition by joining the circus.

"Then I'll make Mr. Job understand that I am to have my full hour of your time; and if I don't get it there 'll be trouble between us."

It would have pleased Toby very well to have had Mr. Castle go out with his long whip just then and make trouble for Mr. Lord; but Mr. Castle had not the time to spare, because of the trouble which he was about to make for Toby, and that he commenced on at once.

"Well, get in here and don't waste any more time," he said, sharply.

Toby looked around curiously for a moment, and, not understanding exactly what he was expected to get in and do, asked, "What shall I do?"

"Pull off your boots, coat, and vest."

Since there was no other course than to learn to ride, Toby wisely concluded that the best thing he could do would be to obey his new master without question; so he began to take off his clothes with as much alacrity as if learning to ride was the one thing upon which he had long set his heart.

Mr. Castle was evidently accustomed to prompt obedience, for he not only took it as a matter of course, but endeavored to hurry Toby in the work of undressing.

With his desire to please, and urged by Mr. Castle's words and the ominous shaking of his whip, Toby's preparations were soon made, and he stood before his instructor clad only in his shirt, trousers, and stockings.

The horse was led around to where he stood, and when Mr. Castle held out his hand to help him to mount Toby jumped up quickly without aid, thereby making a good impression at the start as a willing lad.

"Now," said the instructor, as he pulled down the leathern belt which hung from the rope and fastened it around Toby's waist, "stand up in the saddle, and try to keep there. You can't fall, because the rope will hold you up, even if the horse goes out from under you; but it isn't hard work to keep on if you mind what you are about; and if you don't this whip will help you. Now stand up."

Toby did as he was bid; and as the horse was led at a walk, and as he had the long bridle to aid him in keeping his footing, he had no difficulty in standing during the time that the horse went once around the ring; but that was all.

Mr. Castle seemed to think that this was preparation enough for the boy to be able to understand how to ride, and he started the horse into a canter. As might have been expected, Toby lost his balance, the horse went on ahead, and he was left dangling at the end of the rope, very much like a crab that has just been caught by the means of a pole and line.

Toby kicked, waved his hands, and floun-dered about generally, but all to no purpose, until the horse came round again, and then he made frantic efforts to regain his footing, which efforts were aided—or perhaps it would be more proper to say retarded—by the long lash of Mr. Castle's whip, that played around his legs with merciless severity.

"Stand up! stand up!" cried his instructor, as Toby reeled first to one side and then to the other, now standing erect in the saddle and now dangling at the end of the rope, with the horse almost out from under him.

This command seemed needless, as it was exactly what Toby was trying to do; but as it was given he struggled all the harder, until it seemed to him that the more he tried the less did he succeed.

And this first lesson progressed in about the same way until the hour was over, save that now and then Mr. Castle would give him some good advice, but oftener he would twist the long lash of the whip around the boy's legs with such force that Toby believed the skin had been taken entirely off.

It may have been a relief to Mr. Castle when this first lesson was concluded, and it certainly was to Toby, for he had had all the teaching in horsemanship that he wanted, and he thought, with deepest sorrow, that this would be of daily occurrence during all the time that he remained with the circus.

As he went out of the tent he stopped to speak with his friend the old monkey, and his troubles seemed to have increased when he stood in front of the cage calling, "Mr. Stubbs! Mr. Stubbs!" and the old fellow would not even come down from off the lofty perch where he was engaged in monkey gymnastics with several younger companions. It seemed to him, as he afterward told Ben, "as if Mr. Stubbs had gone back on him because he knew that he was in trouble."

When he went toward the booth Mr. Lord looked at him around the corner of the canvas —for it seemed to Toby that his employer could look around a square corner with much greater ease than he could straight ahead— with a disagreeable leer in his eye, as though he enjoyed the misery which he knew his little clerk had just undergone.

"Can you ride yet?" he asked, mockingly, as Toby stepped behind the counter to attend to his regular line of business.

Toby made no reply, for he knew that the question was only asked sarcastically and not through any desire for information. In a few moments Mr. Lord left him to attend to the booth alone and went into the tent, where Toby rightly conjectured he had gone to question Mr. Castle upon the result of the lesson just given.

That night Old Ben asked him how he had got on while under the teaching of Mr. Castle; and Toby, knowing that the question was asked because of the real interest which Ben had in his welfare, replied:

"If I was tryin' to learn how to swing round the ring, strapped to a rope, I should say that I got along first rate; but I don't know much about the horse, for I was only on his back a little while at a time."

"You'll get over that soon," said Old Ben, patronizingly, as he patted him on the back. "You remember my words, now: I say that you've got it in you, an' if you've a mind to take hold an' try to learn you'll come out on the top of the heap yet, an' be one of the smartest riders they've got in this show."

"I don't want to be a rider," said Toby, sadly; "I only want to get back home once more, an' then you'll see how much it 'll take to get me away again."

"Well," said Ben, quietly, "be that as it may, while you're here the best thing you can do is to take hold an' get ahead just as fast as you can; it 'll make it a mighty sight easier for you while you're with the show, an' it won't spoil any of your chances for runnin' away whenever the time comes."

Toby fully appreciated the truth of this remark, and he assured Ben that he should do all in his power to profit by the instruction given, and to please this new master who had been placed over him.

And with this promise he lay back on the seat and went to sleep, not to awaken until

the preparations were being made for the
entrée into the next town, and Mr. Lord's
harsh voice had cried out his name, with no
gentle tone, several times.

Toby's first lesson with Mr. Castle was
the most pleasant one he had; for after the
boy had once been into the ring his master
seemed to expect that he could do everything
which he was told to do, and when he failed
in any little particular the long lash of the
whip would go curling around his legs or
arms, until the little fellow's body and limbs
were nearly covered with the blue-and-black
stripes.

For three lessons only was the wooden
upright used to keep him from falling; after
that he was forced to ride standing erect on
the broad wooden saddle, or pad, as it is prop-
erly called; and whenever he lost his balance
and fell there was no question asked as to
whether or not he had hurt himself, but he
was mercilessly cut with the whip.

Messrs. Lord and Jacobs gained very much
by comparison with Mr. Castle in Toby's
mind. He had thought that his lot could
not be harder than it was with them; but
when he had experienced the pains of two

or three of Mr. Castle's lessons in horsemanship he thought that he would stay with the
candy venders all the season cheerfully rather
than take six more lessons of Mr. Castle.

Night after night he fell asleep from the
sheer exhaustion of crying, as he had been
pouring out his woes in the old monkey's ears
and laying his plans to run away. Now
more than ever was he anxious to get away,
and yet each day was taking him farther from
home and consequently necessitating a larger
amount of money with which to start. As
Old Ben did not give him as much sympathy as
Toby thought he ought to give—for the old
man, while he would not allow Mr. Job Lord
to strike the boy if he was near, thought it
a necessary portion of the education for Mr.
Castle to lash him all he had a mind to—he
poured out all his troubles in the old monkey's
ears, and kept him with him from the time he
ceased work at night until he was obliged to
commence again in the morning.

The skeleton and his wife thought Toby's
lot a hard one, and tried by every means in
their power to cheer the poor boy. Neither
one of them could say to Mr. Castle what
they had said to Mr. Lord, for the rider was a

far different sort of a person and one whom
they would not be allowed to interfere with
in any way. Therefore poor Toby was obliged
to bear his troubles and his whippings as best
he might, with only the thought to cheer him
of the time when he could leave them all by
running away.

But, despite all his troubles, Toby learned
to ride faster than his teacher had expected
he would, and in three weeks he found little
or no difficulty in standing erect while his
horse went around the ring at his fastest gait.
After that had been accomplished his progress
was more rapid, and he gave promise of becoming a very good rider—a fact which pleased
both Mr. Castle and Mr. Lord very much,
as they fancied that in another year Toby
would be the source of a very good income
to them.

The proprietor of the circus took considerable interest in Toby's instruction, and promised Mr. Castle that Mademoiselle Jeannette
and Toby should do an act together in the
performance just as soon as the latter was
sufficiently advanced. The boy's costume
had been changed after he could ride without
falling off, and now while he was in the ring

165

he wore the same as that used by the regular performers.

The little girl had, after it was announced that she and Toby were to perform together, been an attentive observer during the hour that Toby was under Mr. Castle's direction, and she gave him many suggestions that were far more valuable, and quicker to be acted upon, than those given by the teacher himself.

"To-morrow you two will go through the exercise together," said Mr. Castle to Toby and Ella, at the close of one of Toby's lessons, after he had become so skillful that he could stand with ease on the pad, and even advanced so far that he could jump through a hoop without falling more than twice out of three times.

The little girl appeared highly delighted by this information, and expressed her joy.

"It will be real nice," she said to Toby, after Mr. Castle had left them alone. "I can help you lots, and it won't be very long before we can do an act all by ourselves in the performance, and then won't the people clap their hands when we come in!"

"It 'll be better for you to-morrow than it will for me," said Toby, rubbing his legs

166

sorrowfully, still feeling the sting of the whip. "You see, Mr. Castle won't dare to whip you, an' he 'll make it all count on me, 'cause he knows Mr. Lord likes to have him whip me."

"But I sha'n't make any mistake," said Ella, confidently, "and so you won't have to be whipped on my account; and while I am on the horse you can't be whipped, for he couldn't do it without whipping me, so you see you won't get only half as much."

Toby brightened up a little under the influence of this argument; but his countenance fell again as he thought that his chances for getting away from the circus were growing less each day.

"You see I want to get back to Uncle Dan'l an' Guilford," he said, confidentially; "I don't want to stay here a single minute."

Ella opened her eyes in wide astonishment as she cried: "Don't want to stay here? Why don't you go home, then?"

"'Cause Job Lord won't let me," said Toby, wondering if it was possible that his little companion did not know exactly what sort of a man his master was.

Then he told her—after making her give him all kinds of promises, including the ceremony of crossing her throat, that she would never tell a single soul—that he had had many thoughts, and had formed all kinds of plans for running away. He told her about losing his money, about his friendship for the skeleton and the fat lady, and at last he confided in her that he was intending to take the old monkey with him when he should make the attempt.

She listened with the closest attention, and when he told her that his little hoard had now reached the sum of seven dollars and ten cents—almost as much as he had before — she said, eagerly: "I've got three little gold dollars in my trunk, an' you shall have them all; they're my very own, for mamma gave them to me to do just what I wanted to with them. But I don't see how you can take Mr. Stubbs with you, for that would be stealing."

"No, it wouldn't, neither," said Toby, stoutly. "Wasn't he give to me to do just as I wanted to with? An' didn't the boss say he was all mine?"

"Oh, I'd forgotten that," said Ella, thoughtfully. "I suppose you can take him; but he'll be awfully in the way, won't he?"

"No," said Toby, anxious to say a good

word for his pet; "he always does just what I want him to, an' when I tell him what I'm tryin' to do he'll be as good as anything. But I can't take your dollars."

"Why not?"

"'Cause that wouldn't be right for a boy to let a girl littler than himself help him; I'll wait till I get money enough of my own, an' then I'll go."

"But I want you to take my money, too; I want you to have it."

"No, I can't take it," said Toby, shaking his head resolutely as he put the golden temptation from him; and then, as a happy thought occurred to him, he said, quickly: "I tell you what to do with your dollars: you keep them till you grow up to be a woman, an' when I'm a man I'll come, an' then we'll buy a circus of our own. I think perhaps I'd like to be with a circus if I owned one myself. We'll have lots of money then, an' we can do just what we want to."

This idea seemed to please the little girl, and the two began to lay all sorts of plans for that time when they should be man and woman, have lots of money, and be able to do just what they wanted to.

They had been sitting on the edge of the newly made ring while they were talking, and before they had half finished making plans for the future one of the attendants came in to put things to order, and they were obliged to leave their seats, she going to the hotel to get ready for the afternoon's performance, and Toby to try to do such work as Mr. Job had laid out for him.

Just ten weeks from the time Toby had first joined the circus Mr. Castle informed him and Ella that they were to appear in public on the following day. They had been practicing daily, and Toby had become so skillful that both Mr. Castle and Mr. Lord saw that the time had come when he could be made to earn some money for them.

XV

TOBY'S FRIENDS PRESENT HIM WITH A COSTUME

DURING this time Toby's funds had accumulated rather slower than on the first few days he was in the business, but he had saved eleven dollars, and Mr. Lord had paid him five dollars of his salary, so that he had the to him enormous sum of sixteen dollars; and he had about made up his mind to make one effort for liberty when the news came that he was to ride in public.

He had, in fact, been ready to run away any time within the past week; but, as if they had divined his intentions, both Mr. Castle and Mr. Lord had kept a very strict watch over him, one or the other keeping him in sight from the time he got through with his labors at night until they saw him on the cart with Old Ben.

"I was just gettin' ready to run away," said Toby to Ella on the day Mr. Castle gave his decision as to their taking part in the performance, and while they were walking out of the tent, "an' I shouldn't wonder now if I got away to-night."

"Oh, Toby!" exclaimed the girl, as she looked reproachfully at him, "after all the work we've had to get ready, you won't go off and leave me before we've had a chance to see what the folks will say when they see us together?"

It was impossible for Toby to feel any delight at the idea of riding in public, and he would have been willing to have taken one of Mr. Lord's most severe whippings if he could have escaped from it; but he and Ella had become such firm friends, and he had conceived such a boyish admiration for her, that he felt as if he were willing to bear almost anything for the sake of giving her pleasure. Therefore he said, after a few moments' reflection: "Well, I won't go to-night, anyway, even if I have the best chance that ever was. I'll stay one day more, anyhow, an' perhaps I'll have to stay a good many."

"That's a nice boy," said Ella, positively, as Toby thus gave his decision, "and I'll kiss you for it."

Before Toby fully realized what she was about, almost before he had understood what she said, she had put her arms around his neck and given him a good sound kiss right on his freckled face.

Toby was surprised, astonished, and just a little bit ashamed. He had never been kissed by a girl before—very seldom by anyone, save the fat lady—and he hardly knew what to do or say. He blushed until his face was almost as red as his hair, and this color had the effect of making his freckles stand out with startling distinctness. Then he looked carefully around to see if anyone had seen them.

"I never had a girl kiss me before," said Toby, hesitatingly, "an' you see it made me feel kinder queer to have you do it out here, where everybody could see."

"Well, I kissed you because I like you very much and because you are going to stay and ride with me to-morrow," she said, positively; and then she added, slyly, "I may kiss you again, if you don't get a chance to run away very soon."

"I wish it wasn't for Uncle Dan'l an' the rest of the folks at home, an' there wasn't any such men as Mr. Lord an' Mr. Castle, an'

173

then I don't know but I might want to stay with the circus, 'cause I like you awful much."

And as he spoke Toby's heart grew very tender toward the only girl friend he had ever known.

By this time they had reached the door of the tent, and as they stepped outside one of the drivers told them that Mr. Treat and his wife were very anxious to see both of them in their tent.

"I don't believe I can go," said Toby, doubtfully, as he glanced toward the booth, where Mr. Lord was busy in attending to customers, and evidently waiting for Toby to relieve him, so that he could go to his dinner; "I don't believe Mr. Lord will let me."

"Go and ask him," said Ella, eagerly. "We won't be gone but a minute."

Toby approached his employer with fear and trembling. He had never before asked leave to be away from his work, even for a moment, and he had no doubt but that his request would be refused with blows.

"Mr. Treat wants me to come in his tent for a minute. Can I go?" he asked, in a timid voice, and in such a low tone as to render it almost inaudible.

Mr. Lord looked at him for an instant, and Toby was sure that he was making up his mind whether to kick him or catch him by the collar and use the rubber cane on him. But he had no such intention, evidently, for he said, in a voice unusually mild, "Yes, an' you needn't come to work again until it's time to go into the tent."

Toby was almost alarmed at this unusual kindness, and it puzzled him so much that he would have forgotten he had permission to go away if Ella had not pulled him gently by the coat.

If he had heard a conversation between Mr. Lord and Mr. Castle that very morning he would have understood why it was that Mr. Lord had so suddenly become kind. Mr. Castle had told Job that the boy had really shown himself to be a good rider, and that in order to make him more contented with his lot, and to keep him from running away, he must be used more kindly, and perhaps be taken from the candy business altogether, which latter advice Mr. Lord did not look upon with favor, because of the large sales which the boy made.

When they reached the skeleton's tent they

found, to their surprise, that no exhibition was being given at that hour, and Ella said, with some concern: "How queer it is that the doors are not open! I do hope that they are not sick."

Toby felt a strange sinking at his heart as the possibility suggested itself that one or both of his kind friends might be ill; for they had both been so kind and attentive to him that he had learned to love them very dearly.

But the fears of both the children were dispelled when they tried to get in at the door and were met with the smiling skeleton himself, who said, as he threw the canvas aside as far as if he were admitting his own enormous Lilly:

"Come in, my friends, come in. I have had the exhibition closed for one hour, in order that I might show my appreciation of my friend Mr. Tyler."

Toby looked around in some alarm, fearing that Mr. Treat's friendship was about to be displayed in one of his state dinners, which he had learned to fear rather than enjoy. But as he saw no preparations for dinner he breathed more freely and wondered what all this ceremony could possibly mean.

Neither he nor Ella was long left in doubt, for as soon as they had entered, Mrs. Treat waddled from behind the screen which served them as a dressing room, with a bundle in her arms, which she handed to her husband.

He took it and, quickly mounting the platform, leaving Ella and Toby below, he commenced to speak, with very many flourishes of his thin arms.

"My friends," he began, as he looked down upon his audience of three, who were listening in the following attitudes: Ella and Toby were standing upon the ground at the foot of the platform, looking up with wide-open, staring eyes; and his fleshy wife was seated on a bench which had evidently been placed in such a position below the speaker's stand that she could hear and see all that was going on without the fatigue of standing up, which, for one of her size, was really very hard work— "My friends," repeated the skeleton, as he held his bundle in front of him with one hand and gesticulated with the other, "we all of us know that to-morrow our esteemed and worthy friend Mr. Toby Tyler makes his first appearance in any ring, and we all of us believe that he will soon become a bright and shining light in the profession which he is so soon to enter."

The speaker was here interrupted by loud applause from his wife, and he profited by the opportunity to wipe a stray drop of perspiration from his fleshless face. Then, as the fat lady ceased the exertion of clapping her hands, he continued:

"Knowing that our friend Mr. Tyler was being instructed, preparatory to dazzling the public with his talents, my wife and I began to prepare for him some slight testimonial of our esteem; and, being informed by Mr. Castle some days ago of the day on which he was to make his first appearance before the public, we were enabled to complete our little gift in time for the great and important event."

Here the skeleton paused to take a breath, and Toby began to grow more uncomfortably red in the face. Such praise made him feel very awkward.

"I hold in this bundle," continued Mr. Treat as he waved the package on high, "a costume for our bold and worthy equestrian, and a sash to match for his beautiful and accomplished companion. In presenting these little tokens

my wife (who has embroidered every inch of
the velvet herself) and I feel proud to know
that, when the great and auspicious occasion
occurs to-morrow, the worthy Mr. Tyler will
step into the ring in a costume which we have
prepared expressly for him; and thus, when he
does himself honor by his performance and
earns the applause of the multitude, he will be
doing honor and doing applause for the work
of our hands—my wife Lilly and myself.
Take them, my boy; and when you array
yourself in them to-morrow you will remember
that the only living skeleton, and the wonder
cf the nineteenth century in the shape of the
mammoth lady, are present in their works
if not in their persons."

As he finished speaking Mr. Treat handed
the bundle to Toby, and then joined in the
applause which was being given by Mrs.
Treat and Ella.

Toby unrolled the package, and found that
it contained a circus rider's costume of pink
tights and blue-velvet trunks, collar and cuffs,
embroidered in white and plentifully spangled
with silver. In addition was a wide blue
sash for Ella, embroidered to correspond with
Toby's costume.

The little fellow was both delighted with the gift and at a loss to know what to say in response. He looked at the costume over and over again, and the tears of gratitude that these friends should have been so good to him came into his eyes. He saw, however, that they were expecting him to say something in reply, and, laying the gift on the platform, he said to the skeleton and his wife:

"You've been so good to me ever since I've been with the circus that I wish I was big enough to say somethin' more than that I'm much obliged, but I can't. One of these days, when I m a man, I'll show you how much I like you, an' then you won't be sorry that you was good to such a poor little runaway boy as I am."

Here the skeleton broke in with such loud applause and so many cries of "Hear! hear!" that Toby grew still more confused, and forgot entirely what he was intending to say next.

"I want you to know how much obliged I am," he said, after much hesitation, "an' when I wear 'em I'll ride just the best I know how, even if I don't want to, an' you sha'n't be sorry that you gave them to me."

As Toby concluded he made a funny little

awkward bow, and then seemed to be trying
to hide himself behind a chair from the applause which was given so generously.

"Bless your dear little heart!" said the fat
lady, after the confusion had somewhat subsided. "I know you will do your best, anyway, and I'm glad to know that you're going
to make your first appearance in something
that Samuel and I made for you."

Ella was quite as well pleased with her sash
as Toby was with his costume, and thanked
Mr. and Mrs. Treat in a pretty little way
that made Toby wish he could say anything
half so nicely.

The hour wh'ch the skeleton had devoted
for the purpose of the presentation and accom-
panying speeches having elapsed, it was necessary that Ella and Toby should go and
that the doors of the exhibition be opened at
once, in order to give any of the public an
opportunity of seeing what the placards
announced as two of the greatest curiosities
on the face of the globe.

That day, while Toby performed his ardu-
ous labors, his heart was very light, for the
evidences which the skeleton and his wife had
given of their regard for him were very grati-

fying. He determined that he would do his very best to please so long as he was with the circus, and then, when he got a chance to run away, he would do so, but not until he had said good-by to Mr. and Mrs. Treat and thanked them again for their interest in him.

When he had finished his work in the tent that night Mr. Lord said to him, as he patted him on the back in the most fatherly fashion, and as if he had never spoken a harsh word to him, "You can't come in here to sell candy now that you are one of the performers, my boy; an' if I can find another boy to-morrow you won't have to work in the booth any longer, an' your salary of a dollar a week will go on just the same, even if you don't have anything to do but to ride."

This was a bit of news that was as welcome to Toby as it was unexpected, and he felt more happy then than he had for the ten weeks that he had been traveling under Mr. Lord's cruel mastership.

But there was one thing that night that rather damped his joy, and that was that he noticed that Mr. Lord was unusually careful to watch him, not even allowing him to go outside the tent without following. He saw

at once that, if he was to have a more easy
time, his chances for running away were
greatly diminished, and no number of beautiful costumes would have made him content
to stay with the circus one moment longer
than was absolutely necessary.

That night he told Old Ben the events of the
day, and expressed the hope that he might
acquit himself creditably when he made his
first appearance on the following day.

Ben sat thoughtfully for some time, and
then, making all the preparations which Toby
knew so well signified a long bit of advice, he
said: "Toby, my boy, I've been with a circus,
man an' boy, nigh to forty years, an' I've
seen lots of youngsters start in just as you're
goin' to start in to-morrow; but the most of
them petered out, because they got to knowin'
more 'n them that learned 'em did. Now,
you remember what I say, an' you'll find it
good advice: whatever business you get into,
don't think you know all about it before
you've begun. Remember that you can always learn somethin', no matter how old you
are, an' keep your eyes an' ears open, an' your
tongue between your teeth, an' you'll amount
to somethin', or my name hain't Ben."

14   183

XVI

TOBY'S FIRST APPEARANCE IN THE RING

WHEN the circus entered the town which had been selected as the place where Toby was to make his debut as a circus rider the boy noticed a new poster among the many glaring and gaudy bills which set forth the varied and numerous attractions that were to be found under one canvas for a trifling admission fee, and he noticed it with some degree of interest, not thinking for a moment that it had any reference to him.

It was printed very much as follows:

MADEMOISELLE JEANNETTE
AND
MONSIEUR AJAX

two of the youngest equestrians in the world, will perform their graceful, dashing, and daring act entitled

THE TRIUMPH OF THE INNOCENTS!

This is the first appearance of these daring young riders together since their separation in Europe last season, and their performance in this town will have a new and novel interest. See

MADEMOISELLE JEANNETTE
AND
MONSIEUR AJAX

"Look there!" said Toby to Ben, as he pointed out the poster, which was printed in very large letters, with gorgeous coloring, and surmounted by a picture of two very small people performing all kinds of impossible feats on horseback. "They've got someone else to ride with Ella to-day. I wonder who it can be?"

Ben looked at Toby for a moment, as if to assure himself that the boy was in earnest in asking the question, and then he relapsed into the worst fit of silent laughing that Toby had ever seen. After he had quite recovered he asked: "Don't you know who Monsieur Ajax is? Hain't you never seen him?"

"No," replied Toby, at a loss to understand what there was so very funny in his very natural question. "I thought that I was goin' to ride with Ella."

"Why, that's you!" almost screamed Ben, in delight. "Monsieur Ajax means you— didn't you know it? You don't suppose they would go to put 'Toby Tyler' on the bills, do you? How it would look!—'Mademoiselle Jeannette an' Monsieur Toby Tyler'!"

Ben was off in one of his laughing spells again; and Toby sat there, stiff and straight, hardly knowing whether to join in the mirth or to get angry at the sport which had been made of his name.

"I don't care," he said, at length. "I'm sure I think Toby Tyler sounds just as well as Monsieur Ajax, an' I'm sure it fits me a good deal better."

"That may be," said Ben, soothingly; "but you see it wouldn't go down so well with the public. They want furrin riders, an' they must have 'em, even if it does spoil your name."

Despite the fact that he did not like the new name that had been given him, Toby could not but feel pleased at the glowing terms in which his performance was set off; but he did not at all relish the lie that was told about his having been with Ella in Europe, and he would have been very much better pleased if that portion of it had been left off.

During the forenoon he did not go near Mr. Lord nor his candy stand, for Mr. Castle kept him and Ella busily engaged in practicing the feat which they were to perform in the afternoon, and it was almost time for the performance to begin before they were allowed even to go to their dinner.

Ella, who had performed several years, was very much more excited over the coming debut than Toby was, and the reason why he did not show more interest was, probably, because of his great desire to leave the circus as soon as possible, and during that forenoon he thought very much more of how he should get back to Guilford and Uncle Daniel than he did of how he should get along when he stood before the audience.

Mr. Castle assisted his pupil to dress, and when that was done to his entire satisfaction he said, in a stern voice, "Now you can do this act all right, and if you slip up on it and don't do it as you ought to, I'll give you such a whipping when you come out of the ring that you'll think Job was only fooling with you when he tried to whip you."

Toby had been feeling reasonably cheerful before this, but these words dispelled all his cheerful thoughts, and he was looking more disconsolate when Old Ben came into the dressing tent.

"All ready are you, my boy?" said the old man, in his cheeriest voice. "Well, that's good, an' you look as nice as possible. Now remember what I told you last night, Toby,

an' go in there to do your level best an' make
a name for yourself. Come out here with me
and wait for the young lady."

These cheering words of Ben's did Toby
as much good as Mr. Castle's had the reverse,
and as he stepped out of the dressing room
to the place where the horses were being
saddled Toby resolved that he would do his
very best that afternoon, if for no other reason
than to please his old friend.

Toby was not naturally what might be
called a pretty boy, for his short red hair and
his freckled face prevented any great display
of beauty; but he was a good, honest-looking
boy, and in his tasteful costume looked very
nice indeed—so nice that, could Mrs. Treat
have seen him just then, she would have been
very proud of her handiwork and hugged him
harder than ever.

He had been waiting but a few moments
when Ella came from her dressing room, and
Toby was much pleased when he saw by the
expression of her face that she was perfectly
satisfied with his appearance.

"We'll both do just as well as we can,"
she whispered to him, "and I know the
people will like us and make us come back

after we get through. And if they do
mamma says she'll give each one of us a
gold dollar."

She had taken hold of Toby's hand as she
spoke, and her manner was so earnest and
anxious that Toby was more excited than he
ever had been about his debut; and, had he
gone into the ring just at that moment, the
chances are that he would have surprised
even his teacher by his riding.

"I'll do just as well as I can," said Toby,
in reply to his little companion, "an' if we
earn the dollars I'll have a hole bored in mine,
an' you shall wear it around your neck to
remember me by."

"I'll remember you without that," she
whispered; "and I'll give you mine, so that
you shall have so much the more when you
go to your home."

There was no time for further conversation,
for Mr. Castle entered just then to tell them
that they must go in in another moment.
The horses were all ready—a black one for
Toby, and a white one for Ella—and they
stood champing their bits and pawing the
earth in their impatience until the silver bells
with which they were decorated rang out

quick, nervous little chimes that accorded very well with Toby's feelings.

Ella squeezed Toby's hand as they stood waiting for the curtain to be raised that they might enter, and he had just time to return it when the signal was given, and almost before he was aware of it they were standing in the ring, kissing their hands to the crowds that packed the enormous tent to its utmost capacity.

Thanks to the false announcement about the separation of the children in Europe and their reunion in this particular town, the applause was long and loud, and before it had died away Toby had time to recover a little from the queeer feeling which this sea of heads gave him.

He had never seen such a crowd before, except as he had seen them as he walked around at the foot of the seats, and they they had simply looked like so many human beings; but as he saw them now from the ring they appeared like strange rows of heads without bodies, and he had hard work to keep from running back behind the curtain whence he had come.

Mr. Castle acted as the ringmaster this

time, and after he had introduced them—
very much after the fashion of the posters—
and the clown had repeated some funny joke,
the horses were led in and they were assisted
to mount.

"Don't mind the people at all," said Mr.
Castle, in a low voice, "but ride just as if you
were alone here with me."

The music struck up, the horses cantered
around the ring, and Toby had really started
as a circus rider.

"Remember," said Ella to him, in a low
tone, just as the horses started, "you told
me that you would ride just as well as you
could, and we must earn the dollars mamma
promised."

It seemed to Toby at first as if he could not
stand up, but by the time they had ridden
around the ring once, and Ella had again
cautioned him against making any mistake,
for the sake of the money which they were
going to earn, he was calm and collected
enough to carry out his part of the "act"
as well as if he had been simply taking a
lesson.

The act consisted in their riding side by
side, jumping over banners and through hoops

covered with paper, and then the most difficult
portion began.

The saddles were taken off the horses, and
they were to ride first on one horse and then
on the other, until they concluded their performance by riding twice around the ring
side by side, standing on their horses, each
one with a hand on the other's shoulder.

All this was successfully accomplished without a single error, and when they rode out
of the ring the applause was so great as to
leave no doubt but that they would be recalled
and thus earn the promised money.

In fact, they had hardly got inside the curtain when one of the attendants called to them,
and before they had time even to speak to
each other they were in the ring again, repeating the last portion of their act.

When they came out of the ring for the
second time they found Old Ben, the skeleton,
the fat lady, and Mr. Job Lord waiting to
welcome them; but before anyone could say a
word Ella had stood on tiptoe again and given
Toby just such another kiss as she did when
he told her that he would surely stay long
enough to appear in the ring with her once.

"That's because you rode so well and helped

me so much," she said, as she saw Toby's
cheeks growing a fiery red; and then she
turned to those who were waiting to greet
her.

Mrs. Treat took her in her enormous arms,
and, having kissed her, put her down quickly,
and clasped Toby as if he had been a very
small walnut and her arms a very large pair
of nutcrackers.

"Bless the boy!" she exclaimed, as she
kissed him again and again with an energy
and force that made her kisses sound like the
crack of the whip and caused the horses to
stamp in affright. "I knew he'd amount to
something one of these days, an' Samuel an'
I had to come out, when business was dull,
just to see how he got along."

It was some time before she would unloose
him from her motherly embrace, and when
she did the skeleton grasped him by the hand
and said, in the most pompous and affected
manner:

"Mr. Tyler, we're proud of you, and when
we saw that costume of yours, that my Lilly
embroidered with her own hands, we was
both proud of it and what it contained.
You're a great rider, my boy, a great rider,

and you'll stand at the head of the profession some day, if you only stick to it."

"Thank you, sir," was all Toby had time to say before Old Ben had him by the hand, and the skeleton was pouring out his congratulations in little Miss Ella's ear.

"Toby, my boy, you did well, an' now you'll amount to something, if you only remember what I told you last night," said Ben, as he looked upon the boy whom he had come to think of as his protégé, with pride. "I never seen anybody of your age do any better; an' now, instead of bein' only a candy peddler, you're one of the stars of the show."

"Thank you, Ben," was all that Toby could say, for he knew that his old friend meant every word that he said, and it pleased him so much that he could say no more than "Thank you" in reply.

"I feel as if your triumph was mine," said Mr. Lord, looking benignly at Toby from out his crooked eye, and assuming the most fatherly tone at his command; "I have learned to look upon you almost as my own son, and your success is very gratifying to me."

Toby was not at all flattered by this last praise. If he had never seen Mr. Lord before, he might, and probably would, have been deceived by his words; but he had seen him too often, and under too many painful circumstances, to be at all swindled by his words.

Toby was very much pleased with his success and by the praise he received from all, and when the proprietor of the circus came along, patted him on the head, and told him that he rode very nicely, he was quite happy, until he chanced to see the greedy twinkle in Mr. Lord's eye, and then he knew that all this success and all this praise were only binding him faster to the show which he was so anxious to escape from; his pleasure vanished very quickly, and in its stead came a bitter, homesick feeling which no amount of praise could banish.

It was Old Ben who helped him to undress after the skeleton and the fat lady had gone to their tent and Ella had gone to dress for her appearance with her mother, for now she was obliged to ride twice at each performance. When Toby was in ordinary clothes again Ben said:

"Now that you're one of the performers, Toby, you won't have to sell candy any more, an' you'll have the most of your time to your-

self, so let's you an' I go out an' see the
town."

"Don't you s'pose Mr. Lord expects me to
go to work for him again to-day?"

"An' s'posin' he does?" said Ben, with a
chuckle. "You don't s'pose the boss would
let any one that rides in the ring stand behind
Job Lord's counter, do you? You can do
just as you have a mind to, my boy, an' I say
to you, let's go out an' see the town. What
do you say to it?"

"I'd like to go first-rate, if I dared to,"
replied Toby, thinking of the many whippings
he had received for far less than that which
Ben now proposed he should do.

"Oh, I'll take care that Job don't bother
you, so come along"; and Ben started out of
the tent, and Toby followed, feeling considerably frightened at this first act of dis-
obedience against his old master.

XVII

OFF FOR HOME!

DURING this walk Toby learned many things that were of importance to him, so far as his plan for running away was con-cerned. In the first place, he gleaned from the railway posters that were stuck up in the hotel to which they went that he could buy a ticket for Guilford for seven dollars, and also that, by going back to the town from which they had come, he could go to Guilford by steamer for five dollars.

By returning to this last town—and Toby calculated that the fare on the stage back there could not be more than a dollar—he would have ten dollars left, and that surely ought to be sufficient to buy food enough for two days for the most hungry boy that ever lived.

When they returned to the circus grounds the performance was over, and Mr. Lord in

15   197

the midst of the brisk trade which he usually had after the afternoon performance, and yet, so far from scolding Toby for going away, he actually smiled and bowed at him as he saw him go by with Ben.

"See there, Toby," said the old driver to the boy, as he gave him a vigorous poke in the ribs and then went off into one of his dreadful laughing spells—"see what it is to be a performer an' not workin' for such an old fossil as Job is! He'll be so sweet to you now that sugar won't melt in his mouth, an' there's no chance of his ever attemptin' to whip you again."

Toby made no reply, for he was too busily engaged thinking of something which had just come into his mind to know that his friend had spoken.

But as Old Ben hardly knew whether the boy had answered him or not, owing to his being obliged to struggle with his breath lest he should lose it in the second laughing spell that attacked him, the boy's thoughtfulness was not particularly noticed.

Toby walked around the show grounds for a little while with his old friend, and then the two went to supper, where Toby performed quite as great wonders in the way of eating as he had in the afternoon by riding.

As soon as the supper was over he quietly slipped away from Old Ben, and at once paid a visit to Mr. and Mrs. Treat, whom he found cozily engaged in their supper behind the screen.

They welcomed Toby most cordially, and, despite his assertions that he had just finished a very hearty meal, the fat lady made him sit down to the box which served as table, and insisted on his trying some of her doughnuts.

Under all these pressing attentions it was some time before Toby found a chance to say that which he had come to say, and when he did he was almost at a loss how to proceed; but at last he commenced by starting abruptly on his subject with the words, "I've made up my mind to leave to-night."

"Leave to-night?" repeated the skeleton, inquiringly, not for a moment believing that Toby could think of running away after the brilliant success he had just made. "What do you mean, Toby?"

"Why, you know that I've been wantin' to get away from the circus," said Toby, a little impatient that his friend should be so wonderfully stupid, "an' I think that I'll have as good a chance now as ever I shall, so I'm goin' to try it."

"Bless us!" exclaimed the fat lady, in a gasping way. "You don't mean to say that you're goin' off just when you've started in the business so well? I thought you'd want to stay after you'd been so well received this afternoon."

"No," said Toby—and one quick little sob popped right up from his heart and out before he was aware of it—"I learned to ride because I had to, but I never give up runnin' away. I must see Uncle Dan'l, an' tell him how sorry I am for what I did; an' if he won't have anything to say to me I'll come back; but if he'll let me I'll stay there, an' I'll be *so* good that by 'n' by he'll forget that I run off an' left him without sayin' a word."

There was such a touch of sorrow in his tones, so much pathos in his way of speaking, that good Mrs Treat's heart was touched at once; and putting her arms around the little fellow, as if to shield him from some harm, she said, tenderly: "And so you shall go, Toby, my boy; but if you ever want a home or anybody to love you come right here to us, and you'll never be sorry. So long as Sam keeps thin and I fat enough to draw the public you never need say that you're homeless, for nothing would please us better than to have you come to live with us."

For reply Toby raised his head and kissed her on the cheek, a proceeding which caused her to squeeze him harder than ever.

During this conversation the skeleton had remained very thoughtful. After a moment or two he got up from his seat, went outside the tent, and presently returned with a quantity of silver ten-cent pieces in his hand.

"Here, Toby," he said—and it was to be seen that he was really too much affected even to attempt one of his speeches—"it's right that you should go, for I've known what it is to feel just as you do. What Lilly said about your having a home with us I say, an' here's five dollars that I want you to take to help you along."

At first Toby stoutly refused to take the money; but they both insisted to such a degree that he was actually forced to, and then he stood up to go.

"I'm goin' to try to slip off after Job packs

up the outside booth, if I can," he said, "an'
it was to say good-by that I come around
here."

Again Mrs. Treat took the boy in her arms,
as if it were one of her own children who was
leaving her, and as she stroked his hair back
from his forehead she said: "Don't forget us,
Toby, even if you never do see us again; try
an' remember how much we cared for you,
an' how much comfort you're taking away
from us when you go; for it was a comfort
to see you around, even if you wasn't with us
very much. Don't forget us, Toby, an' if
you ever get the chance, come an' see us.
Good-by, Toby, good-by." And the kind-
hearted woman kissed him again and again,
and then turned her back resolutely upon him,
lest it should be bad luck to him if she again
saw him after saying good-by.

The skeleton's parting was not quite so
demonstrative. He clasped Toby's hand with
one set of his fleshless fingers, while with the
other he wiped one or two suspicious-looking
drops of moisture from his eyes as he said:
"I hope you'll get along all right, my boy,
and I believe you will. You will get home to
Uncle Daniel and be happier than ever, for

now you know what it is to be entirely without a home. Be a good boy, mind your uncle, go to school, and one of these days you'll make a good man. Good-by, my boy."

The tears were now streaming down Toby's face very rapidly; he had not known, in his anxiety to get home, how very much he cared for this strangely assorted couple, and now it made him feel very miserable and wretched that he was going to leave them. He tried to say something more, but the tears choked his utterance and he left the tent quickly to prevent himself from breaking down entirely.

In order that his grief might not be noticed and the cause of it suspected, Toby went out behind the tent, and, sitting there on a stone, he gave way to the tears which he could no longer control.

While he was thus engaged, heeding nothing which passed around him, he was startled by a cheery voice which cried: "Halloo! down in the dumps again? What is the matter now, my bold equestrian?"

Looking up, he saw Ben standing before him, and he wiped his eyes hastily, for here was another from whom he must part and to whom a good-by must be spoken.

Looking around to make sure that no one was within hearing, he went up very close to the old driver and said, in almost a whisper: "I was feelin' bad 'cause I just come from Mr. and Mrs. Treat, an' I've been sayin' good-by to them. I'm goin' to run away to-night."

Ben looked at him for a moment, as if he doubted whether the boy knew exactly what he was talking about, and then said, "So you still want to go home, do you?"

"Oh yes, Ben, *so* much," was the reply, in a tone which expressed how dear to him was the thought of being in his old home once more.

"All right, my boy; I won't say one word ag'in' it, though it do seem too bad, after you've turned out to be such a good rider," said the old man, thoughtfully. "It's better for you, I know; for a circus hain't no place for a boy, even if he wants to stay, an' I can't say but I'm glad you're still determined to go."

Toby felt relieved at the tone of this leave-taking. He had feared that Old Ben, who thought a circus rider was almost on the top-most round of fortune's ladder, would have urged him to stay, since he had made his debut in the ring, and he was almost afraid that he might take some steps to prevent his going.

"I wanted to say good-by now," said Toby, in a choking voice, "'cause perhaps I sha'n't see you again."

"Good-by, my boy," said Ben as he took the boy's hand in his. "Don't forget this experience you've had in runnin' away; an' if ever the time comes that you feel as if you wanted to know that you had a friend, think of Old Ben, an' remember that his heart beats just as warm for you as if he was your father. Good-by, my boy, good-by, an' may the good God bless you!"

"Good-by, Ben," said Toby; and then, as the old driver turned and walked away, wiping something from his eye with the cuff of his sleeve, Toby gave full vent to his tears and wondered why it was that he was such a miserable little wretch.

There was one more good-by to be said, and that Toby dreaded more than all the others. It was to Ella. He knew that she would feel badly to have him go, because she liked to ride the act with him that gave them such applause, and he felt certain that she would urge him to stay.

Just then the thought of another of his friends—one who had not yet been warned of what very important matter was to occur— came to his mind, and he hastened toward the old monkey's cage. His pet was busily engaged in playing with some of the younger members of his family, and for some moments could not be induced to come to the bars of the cage.

At last, however, Toby did succeed in coaxing him forward, and then, taking him by the paw and drawing him as near as possible, Toby whispered, "We're goin' to run away to-night, Mr. Stubbs, an' I want you to be all ready to go the minute I come for you."

The old monkey winked both eyes violently, and then showed his teeth to such an extent that Toby thought he was laughing at the prospect, and he said, a little severely, "If you had as many friends as I have got in the circus you wouldn't laugh when you was goin' to leave them. Of course I've got to go, an' I want to go; but it makes me feel bad to leave the skeleton, an' the fat woman, an' Old Ben, an' little Ella. But I mustn't stand here. You be ready when I come for you, an' by mornin' we'll be so far off that Mr. Lord nor Mr. Castle can't catch us."

The old monkey went toward his companions, as if he were in high glee at the trip before him, and Toby went into the dressing tent to prepare for the evening's performance —which was about to commence.

It appeared to the boy as if everyone was unusually kind to him that night, and, feeling sad at leaving those in the circus who had befriended him, Toby was unusually attentive to everyone around him.   He ran on some trifling errand for one, helped another in his dressing, and in a dozen kind ways seemed as if trying to atone for leaving them secretly.

When the time came for him to go into the ring and he met Ella, bright and happy at the thought of riding with him and repeating her triumphs of the afternoon, nothing save the thought of how wicked he had been to run away from good old Uncle Daniel, and a desire to right that wrong in some way, prevented him from giving up his plan of going back.

The little girl observed his sadness, and she whispered, "Has anyone been whipping you, Toby?"

Toby shook his head. He had thought that he would tell her what he was about to do just before they went into the ring, but her kind words seemed to make that impossible, and he had said nothing when the blare of the trumpets, the noisy demonstrations of the audience, and the announcement of the clown that the wonderful children riders were now about to appear, ushered them into the ring.

If Toby had performed well in the afternoon, he accomplished wonders on this evening, and they were called back into the ring, not once, but twice; and when finally they were allowed to retire everyone behind the curtain overwhelmed them with praise.

Ella was so profuse with her kind words, her admiration for what Toby had done, and so delighted at the idea that they were to ride together, that even then the boy could not tell her what he was going to do, but went into his dressing room, resolving that he would tell her all when they both had finished dressing.

Toby made as small a parcel as possible of the costume which Mr. and Mrs. Treat had given him—for he determined that he would

take it with him—and, putting it under his
coat, went out to wait for Ella. As she did
not come out as soon as he expected, he asked
someone to tell her that he wanted to see her,
and he thought to himself that when she did
come she would be in a hurry and could not
stop long enough to make any very lengthy
objections to his leaving.

But she did not come at all—her mother
sent out word that Toby could not see her
until after the performance was over, owing
to the fact that it was now nearly time for her
to go into the ring, and she was not dressed
yet.

Toby was terribly disappointed. He knew
that it would not be safe for him to wait until
the close of the performance if he were intending to run away that night, and he felt that
he could not go until he had said a few last
words to her.

He was in a great perplexity, until the
thought came to him that he could write a
good-by to her, and by this means any unpleasant discussion would be avoided.

After some little difficulty he procured a
small piece of not very clean paper and a very
short bit of lead pencil, and, using the top of

one of the wagons, as he sat on the seat, for a
desk, he indited the following epistle:

deaR ella I Am goin to Run away two night, & i want
two say good by to yu & your mother. i am Small & unkle
Danil says i dont mount two much, but i am old enuf two
know that you have bin good two me, & when i Am a man
i will buy you a whole cirkus, and we Will ride together.
dont forgit me & i wont yu in haste

TOBY TYLER.

Toby had no envelope in which to seal this
precious letter, but he felt that it would not
be seen by prying eyes and would safely
reach its destination if he intrusted it to Old
Ben.

It did not take him many moments to find
the old driver, and he said, as he handed him
the letter, "I didn't see Ella to tell her I was
goin', so I wrote this letter, an' I want to
know if you will give it to her?"

"Of course I will. But see here, Toby"—
and Ben caught him by the sleeve and led
him aside where he would not be overheard—
"have you got enough money to take you
home? for if you haven't I can let you have
some." And Ben plunged his hand into his
capacious pocket, as if he was about to with-
draw from there the entire United States
Treasury.

Toby assured him that he had sufficient for all his wants; but the old man would not be satisfied until he had seen for himself, and then, taking Toby's hand again, he said: "Now, my boy, it won't do for you to stay around here any longer. Buy something to eat before you start, an' go into the woods for a day or two before you take the train or steamboat. You're too big a prize for Job or Castle to let you go without a word, an' they'll try their level best to find you. Be careful, now, for if they should catch you, good-by any more chances to get away. There"—and here Ben suddenly lifted him high from the ground and kissed him—"now get away as fast as you can."

Toby pressed the old man's hand affectionately, and then, without trusting himself to speak, walked swiftly out toward the entrance.

He resolved to take Ben's advice and go into the woods for a short time, and therefore he must buy some provisions before he started.

As he passed the monkeys' cage he saw his pet sitting near the bars, and he stopped long enough to whisper, "I'll be back in ten minutes, Mr. Stubbs, an' you be all ready then."

Then he went on, and just as he got near the entrance one of the men told him that Mrs. Treat wished to see him.

Toby could hardly afford to spare the time just then, but he would probably have obeyed the summons if he had known that by so doing he would be caught, and he ran as fast as his little legs would carry him toward the skeleton's tent.

The exhibition was open, and both the skeleton and his wife were on the platform when Toby entered; but he crept around at the back and up behind Mrs. Treat's chair, telling her as he did so that he had just received her message and that he must hurry right back, for every moment was important then to him.

"I put up a nice lunch for you," she said as she kissed him, "and you'll find it on the top of the biggest trunk. Now go; and if my wishes are of any good to you, you will get to your uncle Daniel's house without any trouble. Good-by again, little one."

Toby did not dare to trust himself any longer where everyone was so kind to him. He slipped down from the platform as quickly as possible, found the bundle—and a good-sized one it was, too—without any difficulty, and went back to the monkeys' cage.

As orders had been given by the proprietor of the circus that the boy should do as he had a mind to with the monkey, he called Mr. Stubbs; and as he was in the custom of taking him with him at night, no one thought that it was anything strange that he should take him from the cage now.

Mr. Lord or Mr. Castle might possibly have thought it queer had either of them seen the two bundles which Toby carried, but, fortunately for the boy's scheme, they both believed that he was in the dressing tent, and consequently thought that he was perfectly safe.

Toby s hand shook so that he could hardly undo the fastening of the cage, and when he attempted to call the monkey to him his voice sounded so strange and husky that it startled him.

The old monkey seemed to prefer sleeping with Toby rather than with those of his kind in the cage; and as the boy took him with him almost every night, he came on this particular

213

occasion as soon as Toby called, regardless of the strange sound of his master's voice.

With his bundles under his arm and the monkey on his shoulder, with both paws tightly clasped around his neck, Toby made his way out of the tent with beating heart and bated breath.

Neither Mr. Lord, Castle, nor Jacobs were in sight, and everything seemed favorable for his flight. During the afternoon he had carefully noted the direction of the woods, and he started swiftly toward them now, stopping only long enough, as he was well clear of the tents, to say, in a whisper:

"Good-by, Mr. Treat, an' Mrs. Treat, an' Ella, an' Ben. Sometime, when I'm a man, I'll come back an' bring you lots of nice things, an' I'll never forget you—never. When I have a chance to be good to some little boy that felt as bad as I did I'll do it, an' tell him that it was you did it. Good-by."

Then, turning around, he ran toward the woods as swiftly as if his escape had been discovered and the entire company were in pursuit.

XVIII

A DAY OF FREEDOM

TOBY ran at the top of his speed over the rough road; and the monkey, jolted from one side to the other, clutched his paws more tightly around the boy's neck, looking around into his face as if to ask what was the meaning of this very singular proceeding.

When he was so very nearly breathless as to be able to run no more, but was forced to walk, Toby looked behind him, and there he could see the bright lights of the circus and hear the strains of the music as he had heard them on the night when he was getting ready to run away from Uncle Daniel; and those very sounds, which reminded him forcibly of how ungrateful he had been to the old man who had cared for him when there was no one else in the world who would do so, made it more easy for him to leave those behind who had been so kind to him when he stood so much in need of kindness.

"We are goin' home, Mr. Stubbs!" he said, exultantly, to the monkey—"home to Uncle Dan'l an' the boys; an' won't you have a good time when we get there! You can run all over the barn, an' up in the trees, an' do just what you want to, an' there'll be plenty of fellows to play with you. You don't know half how good a place Guilford is, Mr. Stubbs."

The monkey chattered away as if he were anticipating lots of fun on his arrival at Toby's home, and the boy chattered back, his spirits rising at every step which took him farther away from the collection of tents where he had spent so many wretched hours.

A brisk walk of half an hour sufficed to take Toby to the woods, and after some little search he found a thick clump of bushes in which he concluded he could sleep without the risk of being seen by anyone who might pass that way before he should be awake in the morning.

He had not much choice in the way of a bed, for it was so dark in the woods that it was impossible to collect moss or leaves to make a soft resting place, and the few leaves and pine boughs which he did gather made his place for sleeping but very little softer.

216

But during the ten weeks that Toby had been with the circus his bed had seldom been anything softer than the seat of the wagon, and it troubled him very little that he was to sleep with nothing but a few leaves between himself and the earth.

Using the bundle in which was his riding costume for a pillow, and placing the lunch Mrs. Treat had given him near by, where the monkey could not get at it conveniently, he cuddled Mr. Stubbs up to his bosom and lay down to sleep.

"Mr. Lord won't wake us up in the mornin' an' swear at us for not washin' the tumblers," said Toby, in a tone of satisfaction, to the monkey; "an' we won't have to go into the tent to-morrow an' sell sick lemonade an' poor peanuts. But"—and here his tone changed to one of sorrow—"there'll be some there that 'll be sorry not to see us in the mornin', Mr. Stubbs, though they'll be glad to know that we got away all right. But won't Mr. Lord swear, an' won't Mr. Castle crack his whip, when they come to look round for us in the mornin' an' find that we hain't there!"

The reply which the monkey made to this was to nestle his head closer under Toby's coat, and to show, in the most decided manner, that he was ready to go to sleep.

And Toby was quite as ready to go to sleep as he was. He had worked hard that day, but the excitement of escaping had prevented him from realizing his fatigue until after he had lain down; and almost before he had got through congratulating himself upon the ease with which he had gotten free both he and the monkey were as sound asleep as if they had been tucked up in the softest bed that was ever made.

Toby's very weariness was a friend to him that night, for it prevented him from waking; which, if he had done so, might have been unpleasant when he fully realized that he was all alone in the forest, and the sounds that are always heard in the woods might have frightened him just the least bit.

The sun was shining directly in his face when Toby awoke on the following morning, and the old monkey was still snugly nestled under his coat. He sat up rather dazed at first, and then, as he fully realized that he was actually free from all that had made his life such a sad and hard one for so many weeks. he shouted aloud, reveling in his freedom.

The monkey, awakened by Toby's cries, started from his sleep in affright and jumped into the nearest tree, only to chatter, jump, and swing from the boughs when he saw that there was nothing very unusual going on, save that he and Toby were out in the woods again, where they could have no end of a good time and do just as they liked.

After a few moments spent in a short jubilee at their escape Toby took the monkey on his shoulder and the bundles under his arm again, and went cautiously out to the edge of the thicket, where he could form some idea as to whether or no they were pursued.

He had entered the woods at the brow of a small hill when he had fled so hastily on the previous evening, and, looking down, he could see the spot whereon the tents of the circus had been pitched, but not a sign of them was now visible. He could see a number of people walking around, and he fancied that they looked up every now and then to where he stood concealed by the foliage.

This gave him no little uneasiness, for he feared that Mr. Lord or Mr. Castle might be among the number, and he believed that they would begin a search for him at once, and that the spot where their attention would first be drawn was exactly where he was then standing.

"This won't do, Mr. Stubbs," he said, as he pushed the monkey higher up on his shoulder and started into the thickest part of the woods; "we must get out of this place an' go farther down, where we can hide till to-morrow mornin'. Besides, we must find some water where we can wash our faces."

The old monkey would hardly have been troubled if they had not got their faces washed for the next month to come; but he grinned and talked as Toby trudged along, attempting to catch hold of the leaves as they were passed, and in various other ways impeding his master's progress, until Toby was obliged to give him a most severe scolding in order to make him behave himself in anything like a decent manner.

At last, after fully half an hour's rapid walking, Toby found just the place he wanted in which to pass the time he concluded it would be necessary to spend before he dare venture out to start for home.

It was a little valley entirely filled by trees, which grew so thickly, save in one little spot, as to make it almost impossible to walk through. The one clear spot was not more than ten feet square, but it was just at the edge of a swiftly running brook; and a more beautiful or convenient place for a boy and a monkey to stop who had no tent, nor means to build one, could not well be imagined.

Toby's first act was to wash his face, and he tried to make the monkey do the same; but Mr. Stubbs had no idea of doing any such foolish thing. He would come down close to the edge of the water and look in; but the moment that Toby tried to make him go in he would rush back among the trees, climb out on some slender bough, and then swing himself down by the tail, and chatter away as if making sport of his young master for thinking that he would be so foolish as to soil his face with water.

After Toby had made his toilet he unfastened the bundle which the fat lady had given him, for the purpose of having breakfast. As much of an eater as Toby was, he could not but be surprised at the quantity of food which Mrs. Treat called a lunch. There were two whole pies and half of another, as many as two dozen doughnuts, several large pieces of cheese, six sandwiches, with a plentiful amount of meat, half a dozen biscuits, nicely buttered, and a large piece of cake.

The monkey had come down from the tree as soon as he saw Toby untying the bundle, and there was quite as much pleasure depicted on his face, when he saw the good things that were spread out before him, as there was on Toby's; and he showed his thankfulness at Mrs. Treat's foresight by suddenly snatching one of the doughnuts and running with it up the tree, where he knew Toby could not follow.

"Now look here, Mr. Stubbs!" said Toby, sternly, "you can have all you want to eat, but you must take it in a decent way, an' not go to cuttin' up any such shines as that."

And after giving this command—which, by the way, was obeyed just about as well as it was understood—Toby devoted his time to his breakfast, and he reduced the amount of eatables very considerably before he had finished.

Toby cleared off his table by gathering the food together and putting it back into the paper as well as possible, and then he sat down to think over the situation and to decide what he had better do.

He felt rather nervous about venturing out when it was possible for Mr. Lord or Mr. Castle to get hold of him again; and as the weather was yet warm during the night, his camping place everything that could be desired, and the stock of food likely to hold out, he concluded that he had better remain there for two days at least, and then he would be reasonably sure that if either of the men whom he so dreaded to see had remained behind for the purpose of catching him, he would have got tired out and gone on.

This point decided upon, the next was to try to fix up something soft for a bed. He had his pocketknife with him, and in his little valley were pine and hemlock trees in abundance. From the tips of their branches he knew that he could make a bed as soft and fragrant as any that could be thought of, and he set to work at once, while Mr. Stubbs continued his antics above his head.

After about two hours' steady work he had cut enough of the tender branches to make himself a bed into which he and the monkey could burrow and sleep as comfortably as if they were in the softest bed in Uncle Daniel's house.

When Toby first began to cut the boughs

he had an idea that he might possibly make
some sort of a hut; but the two hours' work
had blistered his hands, and he was perfectly
ready to sit down and rest, without the slightest desire for any other kind of a hut than that
formed by the trees themselves.

Toby imagined that in that beautiful place
he could, with the monkey, stay contented
for any number of days; but after he had
rested a time, played with his pet a little,
and eaten just a trifle more of the lunch, the
time passed so slowly that he soon made up
his mind to run the risk of meeting Mr. Lord
or Mr. Castle again by going out of the woods
the first thing the next morning.

Very many times before the sun set that
day was Toby tempted to run the risk that
night, for the sake of the change, if no more;
but as he thought the matter over he saw how
dangerous such a course would be and he
forced himself to wait.

That night he did not sleep as soundly as
on the previous one, for the very good reason
that he was not as tired. He awoke several
times; and the noise of the night birds alarmed
him to such an extent that he was obliged to
awaken the old monkey for company.

But the night passed despite his fears, as all nights will, whether a boy is out in the woods alone or tucked up in his own little bed at home. In the morning Toby made all possible haste to get away, for each moment that he stayed now made him more impatient to be moving toward home.

He washed himself as quickly as possible, ate his breakfast with the most unseemly haste, and, taking up his bundles and the monkey, once more started, as he supposed, in the direction from which he had entered the woods.

Toby walked briskly along, in the best possible spirits, for his running away was now an accomplished fact, and he was going toward Uncle Daniel and home just as fast as possible. He sang "Old Hundred" through five or six times by way of showing his happiness. It is quite likely that he would have sung something a little more lively had he known anything else; but "Old Hundred" was the extent of his musical education, and he kept repeating that, which was quite as satisfactory as if he had been able to go through with every opera that was ever written.

The monkey would jump from his shoulder

into the branches above, run along on the trees for a short distance, and then wait until Toby came along, when he would drop down on his shoulder suddenly, and in every other way of displaying monkey delight he showed that he was just as happy as it was possible.

Toby trudged on in this contented way for nearly an hour, and every moment expected to step out to the edge of the woods, where he could see houses and men once more. But instead of doing so the forest seemed to grow more dense, and nothing betokened his approach to the village. There was a great fear came into Toby's heart just then, and for a moment he halted in helpless perplexity. His lips began to quiver, his face grew white, and his hand trembled so that the old monkey took hold of one of his fingers and looked at it wonderingly.

XIX

TOBY had begun to realize that he was lost in the woods, and the thought was sufficient to cause alarm in the mind of one much older than the boy. He said to himself that he would keep on in the direction he was then traveling for fifteen minutes; and as he had no means of computing the time he sat down on a log, took out the bit of pencil with which he had written the letter to Ella, and multiplied sixty by fifteen. He knew that there were sixty seconds to the minute, and that he could ordinarily count one to each second; therefore, when he learned that there were nine hundred seconds in fifteen minutes he resolved to walk as nearly straight ahead as possible until he should have counted that number.

He walked on, counting as regularly as he could, and thought to himself that he never before realized how long fifteen minutes were.

17   227

It really seemed to him that an hour had passed before he finished counting, and then when he stopped there were no more signs that he was near a clearing than there had been before he started.

"Ah, Mr. Stubbs, we're lost! we're lost!" he cried, as he laid his cheek on the monkey's head and gave way to the lonesome grief that came over him. "What shall we do? Perhaps we won't ever find our way out, but will die here, an' then Uncle Dan'l won't ever know how sorry I was that I ran away."

Then Toby lay right down on the ground and cried so hard that the monkey acted as if it were frightened, and tried to turn the boy's face over, and finally leaned down and licked Toby's ear.

This little act, which seemed so much like a kiss, caused Toby to feel no small amount of comfort, and he sat up again, took the monkey in his arms, and began seriously to discuss some definite plan of action.

"It won't do to keep on the way we've been goin', Mr. Stubbs," said Toby, as he looked full in his pet's face—and the old monkey sat as still and looked as grave as it was possible for him to look and sit—"for we must be going into the woods deeper. Let's start off this way"—and Toby pointed at right angles with the course they had been pursuing—"an' keep right on that way till we come to something, or till we drop right down an' die."

It is fair to presume that the old monkey agreed to Toby's plan; for although he said nothing in favor of it, he certainly made no objections to it, which to Toby was the same as if his companion had assented to it in the plainest English.

Both the bundles and the monkey were rather a heavy load for a small boy like Toby to carry; but he clung manfully to them, walked resolutely on, without looking to the right or to the left, glad when the old monkey would take a run among the trees, for then he would be relieved of his weight, and glad when he returned, for then he had his company, and that repaid him for any labor which he might have to perform.

Toby was in a hard plight as it was; but without the old monkey for a companion he would have thought his condition was a hundred times worse, and would hardly have had the courage to go on as he was going.

On and on he walked, until it seemed to him
that he could really go no farther, and yet
he could see no signs which indicated the end
of the woods, and at last he sank upon the
ground, too tired to walk another step, saying
to the monkey—who was looking as if he
would like to know the reason of this pause,
"It's no use, Mr. Stubbs, I've got to sit down
here an' rest awhile anyhow; besides. I'm
awfully hungry."

Then Toby commenced to eat his dinner,
and to give the monkey his, until the thought
came to him that he neither had any water
nor did he know where to find it, and then,
of course, he immediately became so thirsty
that it was impossible for him to eat any more.

"We can't stand this," moaned Toby to
the monkey; "we've got to have something
to drink, or else we can't eat all these sweet
things, an' I'm so tired that I can't go any
farther. Don't let's eat dinner now, but let's
stay here an' rest, an' then we can keep on
an' look for water."

Toby's resting spell was a long one, for as
soon as he stretched himself out on the ground
he was asleep from actual exhaustion, and did
not awaken until the sun was just setting, and

then he saw that, hard as his troubles had been before, they were about to become, or in fact had become, worse.

He had paid no attention to his bundles when he lay down, and when he awoke he was puzzled to make out what it was that was strewn around the ground so thickly.

He had looked at it but a very short time when he saw that it was what had been the lunch he had carried so far. After having had the sad experience of losing his money he understood very readily that the old monkey had taken the lunch while he slept, and had amused himself by picking it apart into the smallest particles possible, and then strewn them around on the ground where he now saw them.

Toby looked at them in almost speechless surprise, and then he turned to where the old monkey lay, apparently asleep; but as the boy watched him intently he could see that the cunning animal was really watching him out of one half-closed eye.

"Now you have killed us Mr. Stubbs," wailed Toby. "We never can find our way out of here; an' now we hain't got anything to eat, and by to-morrow we shall be starved to

death. Oh dear! wasn't you bad enough
when you threw all the money away, so you
had to go an' do this just when we was in
awful trouble?"

Mr. Stubbs now looked up as if he had just
been awakened by Toby's grief, looked around
him leisurely as if to see what could be the
matter, and then, apparently seeing for the
first time the crumbs that were lying around
on the ground, took up some and examined
them intently.

"Now don't go to makin' believe that you
don't know how they come there," said Toby,
showing anger toward his pet for the first time.
"You know it was you who did it, for there
wasn't anyone else here, an' you can't fool me
by lookin' so surprised."

It seemed as if the monkey had come to the
conclusion that his little plan of ignorance
wasn't the most perfect success, for he walked
meekly toward his young master, climbed
up on his shoulder, and sat there kissing his
ear or looking down into his eyes, until the
boy could resist the mute appeal no longer,
and took him into his arms and hugged him
closely as he said:

"It can't be helped now, I s'pose, an' we

shall have to get along the best way we can; but it was awful wicked of you, Mr. Stubbs, an' I don't know what we're goin' to do for something to eat."

While the destructive fit was on him the old monkey had not spared the smallest bit of food, but had picked everything into such minute shreds that none of it could be gathered up, and everything was surely wasted.

While Toby sat bemoaning his fate and trying to make out what was to be done for food, the darkness, which had just begun to gather when he first awoke, now commenced to settle around, and he was obliged to seek for some convenient place in which to spend the night before it became so dark as to make the search impossible.

Owing to the fact that he had slept nearly the entire afternoon, and also rendered wakeful by the loss he had just sustained, Toby lay awake on the hard ground, with the monkey on his arm, hour after hour, until all kinds of fancies came to him, and in every sound feared he heard someone from the circus coming to capture him, or some wild beast intent on picking his bones.

The cold sweat of fear stood out on his brow,

and he hardly dared to breathe, much more to speak, lest the sound of his voice should betray his whereabouts and thus bring his enemies down upon him. The minutes seemed like hours, and the hours like days, as he lay there, listening fearfully to every one of the night sounds of the forest; and it seemed to him that he had been there very many hours when at last he fell asleep and was thus freed from his fears.

Bright and early on the following morning Toby was awake, and as he came to a realizing sense of all the dangers and trouble that surrounded him he was disposed to give way again to his sorrow; but he said resolutely to himself, "It might be a good deal worse than it is, an' Mr. Stubbs an' I can get along one day without anything to eat; an' perhaps by night we shall be out of the woods, an' then what we get will taste good to us."

He began his walk—which possibly might not end that day—manfully, and his courage was rewarded by soon reaching a number of bushes that were literally loaded down with blackberries. From these he made a hearty meal, and the old monkey fairly reveled in them, for he ate all he possibly could, and then stowed enough in his cheeks to make a good-sized luncheon when he should be hungry again.

Refreshed very much by his breakfast of fruit, Toby again started on his journey with renewed vigor, and the world began to look very bright to him. He had not thought that he might find berries when the thoughts of starvation came into his mind, and, now that his hunger was satisfied, he began to believe that he might possibly be able to live, perhaps for weeks, in the woods solely upon what he might find growing there.

Shortly after he had breakfast he came upon a brook, which he thought was the same upon whose banks he had encamped the first night he spent in the woods, and, pulling off his clothes, he waded into the deepest part and had a most refreshing bath, although the water was rather cold.

Not having any towels with which to dry himself, he was obliged to sit in the sun until the moisture had been dried from his skin and he could put his clothes on once more. Then he started out on his walk again, feeling that sooner or later he would come out all right.

All this time he had been traveling without

any guide to tell him whether he was going straight ahead or around in a circle, and he now concluded to follow the course of the brook, believing that that would lead him out of the forest some time.

During the afternoon he walked steadily, but not so fast that he would get exhausted quickly, and when by the position of the sun he judged that it was noon he lay down on a mossy bank to rest.

He was beginning to feel sad again. He had found no more berries, and the elation which had been caused by his breakfast and his bath was quickly passing away. The old monkey was in a tree almost directly above his head, stretched out on one of the limbs in the most contented manner possible; and as Toby watched him, and thought of all the trouble he had caused by wasting the food, thoughts of starvation again came into his mind, and he believed that he should not live to see Uncle Daniel again.

Just as he was feeling the most sad and lonely, and when thoughts of death from starvation were most vivid in his mind, he heard the barking of a dog, which sounded close at hand.

His first thought was that at last he was saved, and he was just starting to his feet to shout for help when he heard the sharp report of a gun and an agonizing cry from the branches above, and the old monkey fell to the ground with a thud that told he had received his death wound.

All this had taken place so quickly that Toby did not at first comprehend the extent of the misfortune which had overtaken him; but a groan from the poor monkey, as he placed one little brown paw to his breast, from which the blood was flowing freely, and looked up into his master's face with a most piteous expression, showed the poor little boy what a great trouble it was which had now come.

Poor Toby uttered a loud cry of agony, which could not have been more full of anguish had he received the ball in his own breast, and, flinging himself by the side of the dying monkey, he gathered him close to his breast, regardless of the blood that poured over him, and, stroking tenderly the little head that had nestled so often in his bosom, said, over and over again, as the monkey uttered short moans of agony: "Who could have been so cruel? Who could have been so cruel?"

Toby's tears ran like rain down his face, and he kissed his dying pet again and again, as if he would take all the pain to himself.

"Oh, if you could only speak to me!" he cried, as he took one of the poor monkey's paws in his hand, and, finding that it was growing cold with the chill of death, put it on his neck to warm it. "How I love you, Mr. Stubbs! An' now you're goin' to die an' leave me! Oh, if I hadn't spoken cross to you yesterday, an' if I hadn't a'most choked you the day that we went to the skeleton's to dinner! Forgive me for ever bein' bad to you, won't you, Mr. Stubbs?"

As the monkey's groans increased in number, but diminished in force, Toby ran to the brook, filled his hands with water, and held it to the poor animal's mouth.

He lapped the water quickly and looked up with a human look of gratitude in his eyes, as if thanking his master for that much relief. Then Toby tried to wash the blood from his breast; but it flowed quite as fast as he could wash it away, and he ceased his efforts in that direction, and paid every attention to making his friend and pet more comfortable. He took off his jacket and laid it on the ground for the monkey to lie upon; picked a quantity of large green leaves as a cooling rest for his head, and then sat by his side, holding his paws and talking to him with the most tender words his lips—quivering with sorrow as they were—could fashion.

18

XX

HOME AND UNCLE DANIEL

MEANWHILE the author of all this misery had come upon the scene. He was a young man, whose rifle and well-filled game bag showed that he had been hunting, and his face expressed the liveliest sorrow for what he had so unwittingly done.

"I didn't know I was firing at your pet," he said to Toby as he laid his hand on his shoulder and endeavored to make him look up. "I only saw a little patch of fur through the trees, and, thinking it was some wild animal, I fired. Forgive me, won't you, and let me put the poor brute out of his misery?"

Toby looked up fiercely at the murderer of his pet and asked, savagely: "Why don't you go away? Don't you see that you have killed Mr. Stubbs, an' you'll be hung for murder?"

"I wouldn't have done it under any circumstances," said the young man, pitying Toby's grief most sincerely. "Come away and let me put the poor thing out of its agony."

"How can you do it?" asked Toby, bitterly. "He's dying already."

"I know it, and it will be a kindness to put a bullet through his head."

If Toby had been big enough, perhaps there might really have been a murder committed, for he looked up at the man who so coolly proposed to kill the poor monkey after he had already received his death wound that the young man stepped back quickly, as if really afraid that in his desperation the boy might do him some injury.

"Go 'way off," said Toby, passionately, "an' don't ever come here again. You've killed all I ever had in this world of my own to love me, an' I hate you—I hate you!"

Then, turning again to the monkey, he put his hands on each side of his head, and, leaning down, kissed the little brown lips as tenderly as a mother would kiss her child.

The monkey was growing more and more feeble, and when Toby had shown this act of affection he reached up his tiny paws, grasped Toby's finger, half raised himself from the

ground, and then with a convulsive struggle
fell back dead, while the tiny fingers slowly
relaxed their hold of the boy's hand.

Toby feared that it was death, and yet
hoped that he was mistaken; he looked into
the half-open, fast-glazing eyes, put his hand
over his heart, to learn if it were still beating;
and, getting no responsive look from the dead
eyes, feeling no heart throbs from under that
gory breast, he knew that his pet was really
dead, and flung himself by his side in all the
childish abandonment of grief.

He called the monkey by name, implored
him to look at him, and finally bewailed that
he had ever left the circus, where at least his
pet's life was safe, even if his own back received
its daily flogging.

The young man, who stood a silent spectator
of this painful scene, understood everything
from Toby's mourning. He knew that a boy
had run away from the circus, for Messrs.
Lord and Castle had stayed behind one day,
in the hope of capturing the fugitive, and they
had told their own version of Toby's flight.

For nearly an hour Toby lay by the dead
monkey's side, crying as if his heart would
break, and the young man waited until his

grief should have somewhat exhausted itself, and then approached the boy again.

"Won't you believe that I didn't mean to do this cruel thing?" he asked, in a kindly voice. "And won't you believe that I would do anything in my power to bring your pet back to life?"

Toby looked at him a moment earnestly, and then said, slowly, "Yes, I'll try to."

"Now will you come with me, and let me talk to you? For I know who you are, and why you are here."

"How do you know that?"

"Two men stayed behind after the circus had left, and they hunted everywhere for you."

"I wish they had caught me," moaned Toby; "I wish they had caught me, for then Mr. Stubbs wouldn't be here dead."

And Toby's grief broke out afresh as he again looked at the poor little stiff form that had been a source of so much comfort and joy to him.

"Try not to think of that now, but think of yourself and of what you will do," said the man, soothingly, anxious to divert Toby's mind from the monkey's death as much as possible.

"I don't want to think of myself, and I don't care what I'll do," sobbed the boy, passionately.

"But you must; you can't stay here always, and I will try to help you to get home, or wherever it is you want to go, if you will tell me all about it."

It was some time before Toby could be persuaded to speak or think of anything but the death of his pet; but the young man finally succeeded in drawing his story from him, and then tried to induce him to leave that place and accompany him to town.

"I can't leave Mr. Stubbs," said the boy, firmly; "he never left me the night I got thrown out of the wagon an' he thought I was hurt."

Then came another struggle to induce him to bury his pet; and finally Toby, after realizing the fact that he could not carry a dead monkey with him, agreed to it; but he would not allow the young man to help him in any way, or even to touch the monkey's body.

He dug a grave under a little fir tree near by, and lined it with wild flowers and leaves, and even then hesitated to cover the body with the earth. At last he bethought himself

of the fanciful costume which the skeleton
and his wife had given him, and in this he
carefully wrapped his dead pet. He had not
one regret at leaving the bespangled suit,
for it was the best he could command, and
surely nothing could be too good for Mr.
Stubbs.

Tenderly he laid him in the little grave,
and, covering the body with flowers, said,
pausing a moment before he covered it over
with earth, and while his voice was choked
with emotion: "Good-by, Mr. Stubbs, good-
by! I wish it had been me instead of you that
died, for I'm an awful sorry little boy, now
that you're dead!"

Even after the grave had been filled, and a
little mound made over it, the young man
had the greatest difficulty to persuade Toby
to go with him; and when the boy did con-
sent to go at last he walked very slowly away,
and kept turning his head to look back just so
long as the little grave could be seen.

Then, when the trees shut it completely
out from sight, the tears commenced again
to roll down Toby's cheeks, and he sobbed out:
"I wish I hadn't left him. Oh, why didn't
I make him lie down by me? an' then he'd

be alive now; an' how glad he'd be to know
that we was getting out of the woods at last!"

But the man who had caused Toby this
sorrow talked to him about other matters,
thus taking his mind from the monkey's death
as much as possible, and by the time the boy
reached the village he had told his story
exactly as it was, without casting any re-
proaches on Mr. Lord, and giving himself
the full share of censure for leaving his home
as he did.

Mr. Lord and Mr. Castle had remained in
the town but one day, for they were told that
a boy had taken the night train that passed
through the town about two hours after Toby
had escaped, and they had set off at once to
act on that information.

Therefore Toby need have no fears of meeting either of them just then, and he could
start on his homeward journey in peace.

The young man who had caused the monkey's death tried first to persuade Toby to
remain a day or two with him, and, failing
in that, he did all he could toward getting the
boy home as quickly and safely as possible.
He insisted on paying for his ticket on the
steamboat, although Toby did all he could to

prevent him, and he even accompanied Toby to the next town, where he was to take the steamer.

He had not only paid for Toby's ticket, but he had paid for a stateroom for him; and when the boy said that he could sleep anywhere, and that there was no need of such expense, the man replied: "Those men who were hunting for you have gone down the river, and will be very likely to search the boat, when they discover that they started on the wrong scent. They will never suspect that you have got a stateroom; and if you are careful to remain in it during the trip you will get through safely."

Then, when the time came for the steamer to start, the young man said to Toby: "Now, my boy, you won't feel hard at me for shooting the monkey, will you? I would have done anything to bring him back to life, but, as I could not do that, helping you to get home was the next best thing I could do."

"I know you didn't mean to shoot Mr. Stubbs," said Toby, with moistening eyes as he spoke of his pet, "an' I'm sorry I said what I did to you in the woods."

Before there was time to say any more the

warning whistle was sounded, the plank
pulled in, the great wheels commenced to
revolve, and Toby was really on his way to
Uncle Daniel and Guilford.

It was then but five o'clock in the afternoon,
and he could not expect to reach home until
two or three o'clock in the afternoon of the
next day; but he was in a tremor of excitement as he thought that he should walk
through the streets of Guilford once more,
see all the boys, and go home to Uncle Daniel.

And yet, whenever he thought of that home,
of meeting those boys, of going once more to
all those old familiar places, the memory of
all that he had planned when he should take
the monkey with him would come into his
mind and damp even his joy, great as it was.

That night he had considerable difficulty
in falling asleep, but did finally succeed in
doing so; and when he awoke the steamer
was going up the river, whose waters seemed
like an old friend, because they had flowed
right down past Guilford on their way to the
sea.

At each town where a landing was made
Toby looked eagerly out on the pier, thinking
that by chance someone from his home

might be there and he would see a familiar face again. But all this time he heeded the advice given him and remained in his room, where he could see and not be seen; and it was well for him that he did so, for at one of the landings he saw both Mr. Lord and Mr. Castle come on board the boat.

Toby's heart beat fast and furious, and he expected every moment to hear them at the door, demanding admittance, for it seemed to him that they must know exactly where he was secreted.

But no such misfortune occurred. The men had evidently only boarded the boat to search for the boy, for they landed again before the steamer started, and Toby had the satisfaction of seeing their backs as they walked away from the pier. It was some time before he recovered from the fright which the sight of them gave him; but when he did his thoughts and hopes far outstripped the steamer, which, it seemed, was going so slowly, and he longed to see Guilford with an impatience that could hardly be restrained.

At last he could see the spire of the little church on the hill, and when the steamer rounded the point, affording a full view of the town, and sounded her whistle as a signal for those on the shore to come to the pier, Toby could hardly restrain himself from jumping up and down and shouting in his delight.

He was at the gangplank ready to land fully five minutes before the steamer was anywhere near the wharf, and when he recognized the first face on the pier what a happy boy he was!

He was at home! The dream of the past ten weeks was at length realized, and neither Mr. Lord nor Mr. Castle had any terrors for him now.

He ran down the gangplank before it was ready, and clasped every boy he saw there round the neck, and would have kissed them if they had shown an inclination to let him do so.

Of course he was overwhelmed with questions, but before he would answer any he asked for Uncle Daniel and the others at home.

Some of the boys ventured to predict that Toby would get a jolly good whipping for running away, and the only reply which the happy Toby made to that was:

"I hope I will, an' then I'll feel as if I had kinder paid for runnin' away. If Uncle Dan'l will only let me stay with him again he may whip me every mornin', an' I won't open my mouth to holler."

The boys were impatient to hear the story of Toby's travels, but he refused to tell it them, saying:

"I'll go home, an' if Uncle Dan'l forgives me for bein' so wicked I'll sit down this afternoon an' tell you all you want to know about the circus."

Then, far more rapidly than he had run away from it, Toby ran toward the home which he had called his ever since he could remember, and his heart was full almost to bursting as he thought that perhaps he would be told that he had forfeited all claim to it, and that he could never more call it "home" again.

When he entered the old familiar sitting-room Uncle Daniel was seated near the window, alone, looking out wistfully—as Toby thought—across the fields of yellow waving grain.

Toby crept softly in, and, going up to the old man, knelt down and said, very humbly, and with his whole soul in the words, "Oh, Uncle Dan'l! if you'll only forgive me for bein' so wicked an' runnin' away, an' let me stay here again—for it's all the home I ever had—I'll do everything you tell me to, an' never whisper in meetin' or do anything bad."

And then he waited for the words which would seal his fate. They were not long in coming.

"My poor boy," said Uncle Daniel, softly, as he stroked Toby's refractory red hair, "my love for you was greater than I knew, and when you left me I cried aloud to the Lord as if it had been my own flesh and blood that had gone afar from me. Stay here, Toby, my son, and help to support this poor old body as it goes down into the dark valley of the shadow of death; and then, in the bright light of that glorious future, Uncle Daniel will wait to go with you into the presence of Him who is ever a father to the fatherless."

And in Uncle Daniel's kindly care we may safely leave Toby Tyler.

THE END